A Son

Ruskin Bond has been writing for over sixty years, and now has over 120 titles in print—novels, collections of short stories, poetry, essays, anthologies and books for children. His first novel, *The Room on the Roof*, received the prestigious John Llewellyn Rhys Award in 1957. He has also received the Padma Shri (1999), the Padma Bhushan (2014) and two awards from Sahitya Akademi—one for his short stories and another for his writings for children. In 2012, the Delhi government gave him its Lifetime Achievement Award.

Born in 1934, Ruskin Bond grew up in Jamnagar, Shimla, New Delhi and Dehradun. Apart from three years in the UK, he has spent all his life in India, and now lives in Mussoorie with his adopted family.

RUSKIN BOND

A Song of Many Rivers

RUPA

Published by
Rupa Publications India Pvt. Ltd 2016
7/16, Ansari Road, Daryaganj
New Delhi 110002

Sales centres:
Allahabad Bengaluru Chennai
Hyderabad Jaipur Kathmandu
Kolkata Mumbai

ISBN: 978-81-291-4218-4

First impression 2016

10 9 8 7 6 5 4 3 2 1

Printed at Thomson Press India Ltd., Faridabad

Contents

Introduction   vii

A Song of Many Rivers   1

Sacred Shrines Along the Way   19

Wilson's Bridge   31

A Walk through Garhwal   37

Cold Beer at Chutmalpur   48

From the Pool to the Glacier   55

Tremors in the Night   78

Ganga Takes All   81

How Far Is the River?   84

Angry River   88

Ferns in Foliage   117

A Marriage of the Waters   120

Introduction

Far below Landour, where I live, is the Doon valley. And through it, flows the Suswa river. It's a river I have seen since I was a child. It's not one of the great mighty rivers until it meets the Ganga further downstream.

The Ganga emerges from the majestic Himalayas, rushing over rocks and through ravines and winding through valleys till it reaches the plains. In the mountains, while it is still young, it is the Bhagirathi. The paths of the Bhagirathi and the Alaknanda, the two rivers that join to become the Ganga at Devprayag have held me in thrall for decades. I have walked and stayed along these waters. One is blue and restless; the other is greenish and has an air of calm. My special fondness for the Bhagirathi started when I first saw the river, as a young man. Its swift yet deep waters hold out the promise of peace and serenity; and the green forested valleys it runs through and the steep banks on either side dotted with hamlets captured my heart.

Once the Bhagirathi and the Alaknanda become the Ganga the great vault of stories around it becomes larger, much like the volume of water it now carries. Stories from our legends, or those of the people who live along its banks, people who get caught up in its depths, cities and villages that live and die beside it—these are all a part of the river's story too. And as a writer, I find that there is always a story to narrate about these places and people whose lives are touched by the great rivers.

Of course it's not only the Ganga. Every river that flows by, streams that gurgle across my path and little pools and lakes I have been close to have opened up their waters for me to plunge into and find something to write about. Of these stories, some of the most fascinating are the ones about real people who lived near them. The tale of Wilson, who built bridges across the Bhagirathi, and who married a local girl only to betray her later for another woman, leaving a grief-stricken wraith to haunt the bridge forever, is one that had lived on in the forests along the Bhagirathi for almost a century, when I first heard it.

Given how storytellers from every age have loved rivers, it's hardly surprising that legends abound with references to them. Ganga descends and Shiva catches her in his locks; Krishna dives into the depths of the Yamuna to battle with the serpent—these have lived in our collective imagination for centuries. Sometimes they make their way into my stories too. One of my earliest and still popular stories, 'Angry River' has a mysterious boy who appears at a moment of despair and guides Sita through the flood. Perhaps some of us have been fortunate to meet such real-life people too, who have steadied our rocky boats and played their soothing tune when the waters in our life have become a bit too choppy for our liking.

As a lifelong ambler, I have preferred getting to know new places and towns by exploring them on foot. On my travels around the Garhwal region or while walking up to see glaciers I have come to know the forests and streams and rivers and bridges more closely. From these travels were born some of my observations about the life in these mountains. The tough life of the hill people still leaves me astonished. And what about the animals and birds and insects and butterflies one encounters in the hills while following a river upstream and downstream? The pines that give way to the deodars, the rhododendron trees flowering wildly and the many known and perhaps some as yet little known bugs that fly or crawl around these places?

Now, every year I hear of a devastating flood or numerous landslides along the banks of rivers all across the country. Our needs seem to be outstripping the bounties that have been given to us by nature. Somewhere, we need to slow down and stop taking so much from her. It's time to think of giving back, so that many more boys and girls can grow up like me—watching the sun glint on the rippling clear waters of the numerous rivers, big and small, that crisscross this great land.

Ruskin Bond

A Song of Many Rivers

1
Suswa River

When I look down from the heights of Landour to the broad Valley of the Doon far below, I can see the little Suswa river, silver in the setting sun, meandering through fields and forests on its way to its confluence with the Ganga.

The Suswa is a river I knew well as a boy, but it has been many years since I took a dip in its quiet pools or rested in the shade of the tall spreading trees growing on its banks. Now I see it from my windows, far away, dream-like in the mist, and I keep promising myself that I will visit it again, to touch its waters, cool and clear, and feel its rounded pebbles beneath my feet.

It's a little river, flowing down from the ancient Siwaliks and running the length of the valley until, with its sister river the Song, it slips into the Ganga just above the holy city of Haridwar. I could wade across (except during the monsoon when it was in spate) and the water seldom rose above the waist except in sheltered pools, where there were shoals of small fish.

There is a little known and charming legend about the Suswa and its origins, which I have always treasured. It tells us that the Hindu sage, Kasyapa, once gave a great feast to which all the gods were invited. Now Indra, the god of rain, while on his way to the entertainment, happened to meet 60,000 'balkhils' (pygmies) of the Brahmin caste, who were trying in vain to cross a cow's footprint filled with water—to them, a vast lake!

The god could not restrain his amusement. Peals of thunderous laughter echoed across the hills. The indignant Brahmins, determined to have their revenge, at once set to work creating a second Indra, who should supplant the reigning god. This could only be clone by means of penance, fasting and self-denial, in which they persevered until the sweat flowing from their tiny bodies created the 'Suswa' or 'flowing waters' of the little river.

Indra, alarmed at the effect of these religious exercises, sought the help of Brahma, the creator, who taking on the role of a referee, interceded with the priests. Indra was able to keep his position as the rain god.

I saw no pygmies or fairies near the Suswa, but I did see many spotted deer, cheetal, coming down to the water's edge to drink. They are still plentiful in that area.

2
The Nautch Girl's Curse

At the other end of the Doon, far to the west, the Yamuna comes down from the mountains and forms the boundary between the states of Himachal and Uttaranchal. Today, there's a bridge across the river, but many years ago, when I first went across, it was by means of a small cable car, and a very rickety one at that.

During the monsoon, when the river was in spate, the only way across the swollen river was by means of this swaying trolley, which was suspended by a steel rope to two shaky wooden platforms on either bank. There followed a tedious bus journey, during which some sixty-odd miles were covered in six hours. And then you were at Nahan, a small town a little over 3,000 feet above sea level, set amids hill slopes thick with sal and shishann trees. This charming old town links the subtropical Siwaliks to the first foothills of the Himalayas, a unique situation.

The road from Dagshai and Shimla nuns into Nahan from the north. No matter in which direction you look, the view is a fine one. To the south stretches the grand panorama of the plains of Saharanpur and Ambala, fronted by two low ranges of thickly forested hills. In the valley below, the pretty Markanda river winds its way out of the Kadir valley.

Nahan's main street is curved and narrow, but well-made and paved with good stone. To the left of the town is the former Raja's palace. Nahan was once the capital of the state of Sirmur, now part of Himachal Pradesh. The original palace was built some three or four hundred years ago, but has been added to from time to time, and is now a large collection of buildings mostly in the Venetian style.

I suppose Nahan qualifies as a hill station, although it can be quite hot in summer. But unlike most hill stations, which are less than two hundred years old, Nahan is steeped in legend and history.

The old capital of Sirmur was destroyed by an earthquake some seven to eight hundred years ago. It was situated some twenty-four miles from present day Nahan, on the west bank of the Giri, where the river expands into a lake. The ancient capital was totally destroyed, with all its inhabitants, and apparently no record was left of its then ruling family. Little remained of the ancient city, just a ruined temple and a few broken stone figures.

As to the cause of the tragedy, the traditional story is that a nautch girl happened to visit Sirmur, and performed some wonderful feats. The Raja challenged the girl to walk safely over the Giri on a rope, offering her half his kingdom if she was successful.

The girl accepted the challenge. A rope was stretched across the river. But before starting out, the girl promised that if she fell victim to any treachery on the part of the Raja, a curse would fall upon the city and it would be destroyed by a terrible catastrophe.

While she was on her way to successfully carrying out the feat, some of the Raja's people cut the rope. She fell into the river and was drowned. As predicted, total destruction came to the town.

The founder of the next line of the Sirmur Raja came from the Jaisalmer family in Rajasthan. He was on a pilgrimage to Haridwar with his wife when he heard of the catastrophe that had immolated every member of the state's ancient dynasty. He went at once with his wife into the territory, and established a Jaisalmer Raj. The descent from the first Rajput ruler of Jaisalmer stock, some seven hundred years ago, followed from father to son in an unbroken line. And after much intitial moving about, Nahan was fixed upon as the capital.

The territory was captured by the Gurkhas in 1803, but

twelve years later they were expelled by the British after some severe fighting, to which a small English cemetery bears witness. The territory was restored to the Raja, with the exception of the Jaunsar Bawar region.

Six or seven miles north of Nahan lies the mountain of Jaitak, where the Gurkhas made their last desperate stand. The place is worth a visit, not only for seeing the remains of the Gurkha fort, but also for the magnificent view the mountain commands.

From the northernmost of the mountain's twin peaks, the whole south face of the Himalayas may be seen. From west to north you see the rugged prominences of the Jaunsar Bawar, flanked by the Mussoorie range of hills. It is wild mountain scenery, with a few patches of cultivation and little villages nestling on the sides of the hills. Garhwal and Dehra Dun are to the cast, and as you go downhill you can see the broad sweep of the Yamuna as it cuts its way through the western Siwaliks.

3
Gently flows the Ganga

The Bhagirathi is a beautiful river, gentle and caressing (as compared to the turbulent Alaknanda), and pilgrims and others have responded to it with love and respect. The god Shiva released the waters of Goddess Ganga from his locks, and she sped towards the plains in the tracks of Prince Bhagirath's chariot.

> *He held the river on his head*
> *And kept her wandering, where*
> *Dense as Himalaya's woods were spread*
> *The tangles of his hair.*

Revered by Hindus and loved by all, Goddess Ganga weaves her spell over all who come to her. Some assert that the true Ganga (in its upper reaches) is the Alaknanda. Geographically, this may be so. But tradition carries greater weight in the abode of the Gods, and traditionally the Bhagirathi is the Ganga. Of course, the two rivers meet at Devprayag, in the foothills, and this marriage of the waters settles the issue.

I put the question to my friend Dr Sudhakar Misra, from whom words of wisdom sometimes flow; and true to form, he answered: 'The Alaknanda is Ganga, but the Bhagirathi is Ganga-ji.'

She issues from the very heart of the Himalayas. Visiting Gangotri in 1820, the writer and traveller Baillie Fraser noted: 'We are now in the centre of the Himalayas, the loftiest and perhaps the most rugged range of mountains in the world.'

Here, at the source of the river, we come to the realization that we are at the very centre and heart of things. One has an almost primaeval sense of belonging to these mountains and to this valley in particular. For me, and for many who have been here, the Bhagirathi is the most beautiful of the four main river valleys of Garhwal.

The Bhagirathi seems to have everything—a gentle disposition, deep glens and forests, the ultravision of an open valley graced with tiers of cultivation leading up by degrees to the peaks and glaciers at its head.

At Tehri, the big dam slows down Prince Bhagirath's chariot. But upstream, from Bhatwari to Harsil, there are extensive pine forests. They fill the ravines and plateaus, before giving way to yew and cypress, oak and chestnut. Above 9,000 feet the deodar (*devdar*, tree of the gods) is the principal tree. It grows to a little distance above Gangotri, and then gives way to the birch, which is found in patches to within half a mile of the glacier.

It was the valuable timber of the deodar that attracted the adventurer Frederick 'Pahari' Wilson to the valley in the 1850s. He leased the forests from the Raja of Tehri, and within a few years he had made a fortune. From his horse and depot at Harsil, he would float the logs downstream to Tehri, where they would be sawn up and despatched to buyers in the cities.

Bridge-building was another of Wilson's ventures. The most famous of these was a 350 feet suspension bridge at Bhaironghat, over 1,200 feet above the young Bhagirathi where it thunders through a deep defile. This rippling contraption was at first a source of terror to travellers, and only a few ventured across it.

To reassure people, Wilson would mount his horse and gallop to and fro across the bridge. It has since collapsed, but local people will tell you that the ghostly hoof beats of Wilson's horse can still be heard on full moon nights. The supports of the old bridge were massive deodar trunks, and they can still be seen to one side of the new road bridge built by engineers of the Northern Railway.

The old forest rest houses at Dharasu, Bhatwari and Harsil were all built by Wilson as staging posts, for the only roads were narrow tracks linking one village to another. Wilson married a local girl, Gulabi, from the village of Mukhba, and the portraits of the Wilsons (early examples of the photographer's art) still hang in these sturdy little bungalows. At any rate, I found their pictures at Bhatwari. Harsil is now out of bounds to civilians, and I believe part of the old house was destroyed in a fire a few years ago. This sturdy building withstood the earthquake which devastated the area in 1991.

Amongst other things, Wilson introduced the apple into this area, 'Wilson apples'—large, red and juicy—sold to travellers and pilgrims on their way to Gangotri. This fascinating man also acquired an encyclopaedic knowledge of the wildlife of the region, and his articles, which appeared in *Indian Sporting Life* in the 1860s, were later plundered by so-called wildlife writers for their own works.

He acquired properties in Dehra Dun and Mussoorie, and his wife lived there in some style, giving him three sons. Two died young. The third, Charlie Wilson, went through most of his father's fortune. His grave lies next to my grandfather's grave in the old Dehra Dun cemetery. Gulabi is buried in Mussoorie, next to her husband. I wrote this haiku for her:

> *Her beauty brought her fame,*
> *But only the wild rose growing beside her grave*
> *Is there to hear her whispered name—*
> *Gulabi.*

I remember old Mrs Wilson, Charlie's widow, when I was a boy in Dehra. She lived next door in what was the last of the Wilson properties. Her nephew, Geoffrey Davis, went to school with me in Shimla, and later joined the Indian Air Force. But luck never went the way of Wilson's descendants, and Geoffrey died when his plane crashed.

Wilson's life is fit subject for a romance; but even if one were never written, his legend would live on, as it has done for over a hundred years. There has never been any attempt to commemorate him, but people in the valley still speak of him in awe and admiration, as though he had lived only yesterday.

Some men leave a trail of legend behind them because they give their spirit to the place where they have lived, and remain forever a part of the rocks and mountain streams.

Gangotri is situated at just a little over 10,300 feet. On the right bank of the river is the Gangotri temple, a small neat building without too much ornamentation, built by Amar Singh Thapa, a Nepali General, early in the nineteenth century. It was renovated by the Maharaja of Jaipur in the 1920s. The rock on which it stands is called Bhagirath Shila and is said to be the place where Prince Bhagirath did penance in order that Ganga be brought down from her abode of eternal snow. Here the rocks are carved and polished by ice and water, so smooth that in places they look like rolls of silk. The fast flowing waters of this mountain torrent look very different from the huge sluggish river that finally empties its waters into the Bay of Bengal fifteen hundred miles away.

The river emerges from beneath a great glacier, thickly studded with enormous loose rocks and earth. The glacier is about a mile in width and extends upwards for many miles. The chasm in the glacier through which the stream rushed forth into the light of day is named Gaumukh, the cow's mouth, and is held in deepest reverence by Hindus. The regions of eternal frost in the vicinity were the scene of many of their most sacred mysteries.

The Ganga enters the world no puny stream, but bursts from its icy womb a river thirty or forty yards in breadth. At Gauri Kund (below the Gangotri temple) it falls over a rock of

considerable height and continues tumbling over a succession
of small cascades until it enters the Bhaironghati gorge.

A night spent beside the river, within the sound of the fall,
is an eerie experience. After some time it begins to sound, not
like one fall but a hundred, and this sound permeates both
one's dreams and waking hours. Rising early to greet the dawn
proved rather pointless at Gangotri, for the surrounding peaks
did not let the sun in till after 9 a.m. Everyone rushed about
to keep warm, exclaiming delightedly at what they call 'gulabi
thand', literally, 'rosy cold'. Guaranteed to turn the cheeks a
rosy pink! A charming expression, but I prefer a rosy sunburn,
and remained beneath a heavy quilt until the sun came up to
throw its golden shafts across the river.

This is mid-October, and after Diwali the shrine and the
small township will close for winter, the pandits retreating to the
relative warmth of Mukbha. Soon snow will cover everything,
and even the hardy purple-plumaged whistling thrushes, lovers
of deep shade, will move further down the valley. And down
below the forest-line, the Garhwali farmers go about harvesting
their terraced fields which form patterns of yellow, green and
gold above the deep green of the river.

Yes, the Bhagirathi is a green river. Although deep and swift,
it does not lose its serenity. At no place does it look hurried or
confused—unlike the turbulent Alaknanda, fretting and frothing
as it goes crashing down its boulder-strewn bed. The Alaknanda
gives one a feeling of being trapped, because the river itself is
trapped. The Bhagirathi is free-flowing, easy. At all times and
places it seems to find its true level.

In the old days, only the staunchest of pilgrims visited

the shrines at Gangotri and Jamnotri. The roads were rocky and dangerous, winding along in some places, ascending and descending the faces of deep precipices and ravines, at times leading along banks of loose earth where landslides had swept the original path away.

There are still no large towns above Uttarkashi, and this absence of large centres of population may be reason why the forests are better preserved than those in the Alaknanda valley, or further downstream. Uttarkashi, though a large and growing town, is as yet uncrowded. The seediness of towns like Rishikesh and parts of Dehra Dun is not yet evident here. One can take a leisurely walk through its long (and well-supplied) bazaar, without being jostled by crowds or knocked over by three-wheelers. Here, too, the river is always with you, and you must live in harmony with its sound as it goes rushing and humming along its shingly bed.

Uttarkashi is not without its own religious and historical importance, although all traces of its ancient town of Barahat appear to have vanished. There are four important temples here, and on the occasion of Makar Sankranti, early in January a week-long fair is held when thousands from the surrounding areas throng the roads to the town. To the beating of drums and blowing of trumpets, the gods and goddesses are brought to the fair in gaily decorated palanquins. The surrounding villages wear a deserted look that day as everyone flocks to the temples and bathing ghats and to the entertainments of the fair itself.

We have to move far downstream to reach another large centre of population, the town of Tehri, and this is a very different place from Uttarkashi. Tehri has all the characteristics of a small town in the plains—crowds, noise, traffic congestion, dust and refuse, scruffy dhabas—with this difference that here it is all ephemeral, for Tehri is destined to be submerged by the water of the Bhagirathi when the Tehri dam is finally completed.

The rulers of Garhwal were often changing their capitals, and when, after the Gurkha War (of 1811-15), the former capital of Srinagar became part of British Garhwal, Raja Sudershan Shah established his new capital at Tehri. It is said that when he reached this spot, his horse refused to go any further. This was enough for the king, it seems; or so the story goes.

Perhaps Prince Bhagirath's chariot will come to a halt here too, when the dam is built. The two hundred and forty-six metre high earthen dam, with forty-two square miles of reservoir capacity, will submerge the town and about thirty villages.

But as we leave the town and cross the narrow bridge over the river, a mighty blast from above sends rocks hurtling down the defile, just to remind us that work is indeed in progress.

Unlike the Raja's horse, I have no wish to be stopped in my tracks at Tehri. There are livelier places upstream. And as for Ganga herself, that deceptively gentle river, I wonder if she will take kindly to our efforts to contain her.

4
Falling for Mandakini

A great river at its confluence with another great river is, for me, a special moment in time. And so it was with the Mandakini at Rudraprayag, where its waters joined the waters of the Alaknanda, the one having come from the glacial snows above Kedarnath, the other from the Himalayan heights beyond

Badrinath. Both sacred rivers, destined to become the holy Ganga further downstream.

I fell in love with the Mandakini at first sight. Or was it the valley that I fell in love with? I am not sure, and it doesn't really matter. The valley is the river.

While the Alaknanda valley, especially in its higher reaches, is a deep and narrow gorge where precipitous outcrops of rock hang threateningly over the traveller, the Mandakini valley is broader, gentler, the terraced fields wider, the banks of the river a green sward in many places. Somehow, one does not feel that one is at the mercy of the Mandakini whereas one is always at the mercy of the Alaknanda with its sudden floods.

Rudraprayag is hot. It is probably a pleasant spot in winter, but at the end of June, it is decidedly hot. Perhaps its chief claim to fame is that it gave its name to the dreaded man-eating leopard of Rudraprayag, who in the course of seven years (1918-25) accounted for more than 300 victims. It was finally shot by Jim Corbett, who recounted the saga of his long hunt for the killer in his fine book, *The Man-eating Leopard of Rudraprayag*.

The place at which the leopard was shot was the village of Gulabrai, two miles south of Rudraprayag. Under a large mango tree stands a memorial raised to Jim Corbett by officers and Men of the Border Roads Organisation. It is a touching gesture to one who loved Garhwal and India. Unfortunately, several buffaloes are tethered close by, and one has to wade through slush and buffalo dung to get to the memorial stone. A board tacked on to the mango tree attracts the attention of motorists who might pass without noticing the memorial, which is off to one side.

The killer leopard was noted for its direct method of attack on humans; and, in spite of being poisoned, trapped in a cave, and shot at innumerable times, it did not lose its contempt for man. Two English sportsmen covering both ends to the old suspension bridge over the Alaknanda fired several times at the man-eater but to little effect.

It was not long before the leopard acquired a reputation among the hill folk for being an evil spirit. A sadhu was suspected of turning into the leopard by night, and was only saved from being lynched by the ingenuity of Philip Mason, then deputy commissioner of Garhwal. Mason kept the sadhu in custody until the leopard made his next attack, thus proving the man innocent. Years later, when Mason turned novelist and (using the pen name Philip Woodruffe) wrote *The Wild Sweet Witch*, he had one of the characters, a beautiful young woman who apparently turns into a man-eating leopard by night.

Corbett's host at Gulabrai was one of the few who survived an encounter with the leopard. It left him with a hole in his throat. Apart from being a superb story teller, Corbett displayed great compassion for people from all walks of life and is still a legend in Garhwal and Kumaon amongst people who have never read his books.

In June, one does not linger long in the steamy heat of Rudraprayag. But as one travels up the river, making a gradual ascent of the Mandakini valley, there is a cool breeze coming down from the snows, and the smell of rain is in the air.

The thriving little township of Agastmuni spreads itself along the wide river banks. Further upstream, near a little place called Chandrapuri, we cannot resist breaking our journey to sprawl on the tender green grass that slopes gently clown to the swift flowing river. A small rest house is in the making. Around it, banana fronds sway and poplar leaves dance in the breeze.

This is no sluggish river of the plains, but a fast moving current, tumbling over rocks, turning and twisting in its efforts to discover the easiest way for its frothy snow-fed waters to escape the mountains. Escape is the word! For the constant plaint of many a Garliwali is that, while his hills abound in rivers, the water runs down and away, and little if any reaches the fields and villages above it. Cultivation must depend on the rain and not on the river.

The road climbs gradually, still keeping to the river. Just outside Guptakashi, my attention is drawn to a clump of huge trees sheltering a small but ancient temple. We stop here and enter the shade of the trees.

The temple is deserted. It is a temple dedicated to Shiva, and in the courtyard are several river-rounded stone *lingarns* on which leaves and blossoms have fallen. No one seems to come here, which is strange, since it is on the pilgrim route. Two boys from a neighbouring field leave their yoked bullock to come and talk to me, but they cannot tell me much about the temple except to confirm that it is seldom visited. 'The buses do not stop here.' That seems explanation enough. For where the buses go, the pilgrims go; and where the pilgrims go, other pilgrims will follow. Thus far and no further.

The trees seem to be magnolias. But I have never seen magnolia trees grow to such huge proportions. Perhaps they are something else. Never mind; let them remain a mystery.

Guptakashi in the evening is all a bustle. A coachload of pilgrims (headed for Kedarnath) has just arrived, and the tea- shops near the bus-stand are doing brisk business. Then the 'local' bus from Ukhimath, across the river arrives, and many of the passengers head for a tea shop famed for its *samosas*. The local bus is called the *Bhook Hartal*, the 'Hunger-strike' bus.

'How did it get that name?' I asked one of the samosa-eaters.

'Well, it's an interesting story. For a long time we had been asking the authorities to provide a bus service for the local people and for the villagers who live off the roads. All the buses came from Srinagar or Rishikesh, and were taken up by pilgrims. The locals couldn't find room in them. But our pleas went unheard until the whole town, or most of it, decided to go on hunger-strike.'

'They nearly put me out of business too,' said the tea shop owner cheerfully. 'Nobody ate any samosas for two days!'

There is no cinema or public place of entertainment at Guptakashi, and the town goes to sleep early. And wakes early.

At six, the hillside, green from recent rain, sparkles in the morning sunshine. Snowcapped Chaukhamba (7,140 metres) is dazzling. The air is clear; no smoke or dust up here. The climate, I am told, is mild all the year round judging by the scent and shape of the flowers, and the boys call them Champs, Hindi for champa blossom. Ukhimath, on the other side of the river, lies in the shadow. It gets the sun at nine. In winter, it must wait till afternoon.

Guptakashi has not yet been rendered ugly by the barrack-type architecture that has come up in some growing hill towns.

The old double storeyed houses are built of stone, with gray slate roofs. They blend well with the hillside. Cobbled paths meander through the old bazaar.

One of these takes up to the famed Guptakashi temple, tucked away above the old part of the town. Here, as in Benaras, Shiva is worshipped as Vishwanath, and two underground streams representing the sacred Jamuna and Bhagirathi rivers feed the pool sacred to the God. This temple gives the town its name, Gupta-Kashi, the 'Invisible Benaras', just as Uttarkashi on the Bhagirathi is 'Upper Benaras'.

Guptakashi and its environs have so many *linganis* that the saying *'June Kanhar Utne Shanhar'*—'As many stones, so many Shivas'—has become a proverb to describe its holiness.

From Guptakashi, pilgrims proceed north to Kedarnath, and the last stage of their journey—about a day's march—must be covered on foot or horseback. The temple of Kedarnath, situated at a height of 11.753 feet, is encircled by snowcapped peaks, and Atkinson has conjectured that 'the symbol of the *linga* may have arisen front the pointed peaks around his (God Shiva's) original home.'

The temple is dedicated to Sadashiva, the subterranean form of the God, who, 'fleeing from the Pandavas took refuge here in the form of a he-buffalo and finding himself hard- pressed, dived into the ground leaving the hinder parts on the surface, which continue to be the subject of adoration.' (Atkinson).

The other portions of the God are worshipped as follows: the arms at Tunguath, at a height of 13,000 feet, the face at Rudranath (12,000 feet), the belly at Madmaheshwar, 18 miles northeast of Guptakashi; and the hair and head at Kalpeshwar, near Joshimath. These five sacred shrines form the *Punch Kedar* (five Kedars).

We leave the Mandakini to visit Tungnath on the Chandrashila range. But I will return to this river. It has captured my mind and heart.

Sacred Shrines Along the Way

Nandprayag: Where Rivers Meet

It's a funny thing, but long before I arrive at a place I can usually tell whether I am going to like it or not.

Thus, while I was still some twenty miles from the town of Pauri, I felt it was not going to be my sort of place; and sure enough, it wasn't. On the other hand, while Nandprayag was still out of sight, I knew I was going to like it. And I did. Perhaps it's something on the wind-emanations of an atmosphere that are carried to me well before I arrive at my destination. I can't really explain it, and no doubt it is silly to make judgements in advance. But it happens and I mention the fact for what it's worth.

As for Nandprayag, perhaps I'd been there in some previous existence, I felt I was nearing home as soon as we drove into this cheerful roadside hamlet, some little way above the Nandakini's confluence with the Alakananda river. A prayag is a meeting place of two rivers, and as there are many rivers in the Garhwal

Himalayas, all linking up to join either the Ganga or the Jamuna, it follows that there are numerous prayags, in themselves places of pilgrimage as well as wayside halts enroute to the higher Hindu shrines at Kedarnath and Badrinath. Nowhere else in the Himalayas are there so many temples, sacred streams, holy places and holy men.

Some little way above Nandprayag's busy little bazaar, is the tourist rest-house, perhaps the nicest of the tourist lodges in this region. It has a well-kept garden surrounded by fruit trees and is a little distance from the general hubbub of the main road.

Above it is the old pilgrim path, on which you walked. Just a few decades ago, if you were a pilgrim intent on finding salvation at the abode of the gods, you travelled on foot all the way from the plains, covering about 200 miles in a couple of months. In those days people had the time, the faith and the endurance. Illness and misadventure often dogged their footsteps, but what was a little suffering if at the end of the day they arrived at the very portals of heaven? Some did not survive to make the return journey. Today's pilgrims may not be lacking in devotion, but most of them do expect to come home again.

Along the pilgrim path are several handsome old houses, set among mango trees and the fronds of the papaya and banana. Higher up the hill the pine forests commence, but down here it is almost subtropical. Nandprayag is only about 3,000 feet above sea level—a height at which the vegetation is usually quite lush provided there is protection from the wind.

In one of these double-storeyed houses lives Mr Devki Nandan, scholar and recluse. He welcomes me into his house and plies me with food till I am close to bursting. He has a great love for his little corner of Garhwal and proudly shows me his collection of clippings concerning this area. One of them is from a travelogue by Sister Nivedita—an Englishwoman, Margaret Noble, who became an interpreter of Hinduism to the West. Visiting Nandprayag in 1928, she wrote:

> Nandprayag is a place that ought to be famous for its beauty and order. For a mile or two before reaching it we had noticed the superior character of the agriculture and even some careful gardening of fruits and vegetables. The peasantry also, suddenly grew handsome, not unlike the Kashmiris. The town itself is new, rebuilt since the Gohna flood, and its temple stands far out across the fields on the shore of the Prayag. But in this short time a wonderful energy has been at work on architectural carvings, and the little place is full of gemlike beauties. Its temple is dedicated to Naga Takshaka. As the road crosses the river, I noticed two or three old Pathan tombs, the only traces of Mohammedanism that we had seen north of Srinagar in Garhwal.

Little has changed since Sister Nivedita's visit, and there is still a small and thriving Pathan population in Nandprayag. In fact, when I called on Mr Devki Nandan, he was in the act of sending out Eid greetings to his Muslim friends. Some of the old graves have disappeared in the debris from new road cuttings: an endless business, this road-building. And as for the beautiful temple described by Sister Nivedita, I was sad to learn that it had been swept away by a mighty flood in 1970, when a cloudburst and subsequent landslide on the Alakananda resulted in great destruction downstream.

Mr Nandan remembers the time when he walked to the small hill station of Pauri to join the old Messmore Mission School, where so many famous sons of Garhwal received their early education. It would take him four days to get to Pauri. Now it is just four hours by bus. It was only after the Chinese invasion of 1962 that there was a rush of road-building in the hill districts of northern India. Before that, everyone walked and thought nothing of it!

Sitting alone that same evening in the little garden of the rest-house, I heard innumerable birds break into song. I did not see any of them, because the light was fading and the trees were dark, but there was the rather melancholy call of the hill dove, the insistent ascending trill of the koel, and much shrieking, whistling and twittering that I was unable to assign to any particular species.

Now, once again, while I sit on the lawn surrounded by zinnias in full bloom, I am teased by that feeling of having been here before, on this lush hillside, among the pomegranates and oleanders. Is it some childhood memory asserting itself? But as a child I never travelled in these parts.

True, Nandprayag has some affinity with parts of the Doon Valley before it was submerged by a tidal wave of humanity. But in the Doon there is no great river running past your garden. Here there are two, and they are also part of this feeling of belonging. Perhaps in some former life I did come this way, or maybe I dreamed about living here. Who knows? Anyway, mysteries are more interesting than certainties. Presently the room-boy joins me for a chat on the lawn. He is in fact running the rest-house in the absence of the manager. A coachload of pilgrims is due at any moment but until they arrive the place is empty and only the birds can be heard. His name is Janakpal and he tells me something about his village on the next mountain, where a leopard has been carrying off goats and cattle. He doesn't think much of the conservationists' law protecting leopards: nothing can be done unless the animal becomes a man-eater!

A shower of rain descends on us, and so do the pilgrims, Janakpal leaves me to attend to his duties. But I am not left alone for long. A youngster with a cup of tea appears. He wants me to take him to Mussoorie or Delhi. He is fed up, he says, with washing dishes here.

'You are better off here,' I tell him sincerely. 'In Mussoorie you will have twice as many dishes to wash. In Delhi, ten times as many.'

'Yes, but there are cinemas there,' he says, 'and television, and videos.' I am left without an argument. Birdsong may have charms for me but not for the restless dishwasher in Nandprayag.

The rain stops and I go for a walk. The pilgrims keep to themselves but the locals are always ready to talk. I remember a saying (and it may have originated in these hills), which goes: 'All men are my friends. I have only to meet them.' In these hills, where life still moves at a leisurely and civilized pace, one is constantly meeting them.

The Magic of Tungnath

The mountains and valleys of Uttaranchal never fail to spring surprises on the traveller in search of the picturesque. It is impossible to know every corner of the Himalayas, which means that there are always new corners to discover; forest or meadow, mountain stream or wayside shrine.

The temple of Tungnath, at a little over 12,000 feet, is the highest shrine on the inner Himalayan range. It lies just below the Chandrashila peak. Some way off the main pilgrim routes, it is less frequented than Kedarnath or Badrinath, although it forms a part of the Kedar temple establishment. The priest here is a local man, a Brahmin from the village of Maku; the other Kedar temples have South Indian priests, a tradition begun by Sankaracharya, the eighth century Hindu reformer and revivalist.

Tungnath's lonely eminence gives it a magic of its own. To get there (or beyond), one passes through some of the most delightful temperate forests in the Garhwal Himalayas. Pilgrim, or trekker, or just plain rambler such as myself, one comes away a better person, forest-refreshed, and more aware of what the world was really like before mankind began to strip it bare.

Duiri Tal, a small lake, lies cradled on the hill above Okhimath, at a height of 8,000 feet. It was a favourite spot of one of Garhwal's earliest British Commissioners, J. H. Batten, whose administration continued for twenty years (1836-56). He wrote:

> The day I reached there, it was snowing and young trees were laid prostrate under the weight of snow; the lake was frozen over to a depth of about two inches. There was no human habitation, and the place looked

a veritable wilderness. The next morning when the sun appeared, the Chaukhamba and many other peaks extending as far as Kedarnath seemed covered with a new quilt of snow, as if close at hand. The whole scene was so exquisite that one could not tire of gazing at it for hours. I think a person who has a subdued settled despair in his mind would all of a sudden feel a kind of bounding and exalting cheerfulness which will be imparted to his frame by the atmosphere of Duiri Tal.

This feeling of uplift can be experienced almost anywhere along the Tungnath range. Duiri Tal is still some way off the beaten track, and anyone wishing to spend the night there should carry a tent; but further along this range, the road ascends to Dugalbeta (at about 9,000 feet) where a PWD rest-house, gaily painted, has come up like some exotic orchid in the midst of a lush meadow topped by excelsia pines and pencil cedars. Many an official who has stayed here has rhapsodised on the charms of Dugalbeta; and if you are unofficial (and therefore not entitled to stay in the bungalow), you can move on to Chopta, lusher still, where there is accommodation of a sort for pilgrims and other hardy souls. Two or three little tea-shops provide mattresses and quilts. The Garhwal Mandal is putting up a rest-house. These tourist rest-houses of Garhwal are a great boon to the traveller; but during the pilgrim season (May/June) they are filled to overflowing, and if you turn up unexpectedly you might have to take your pick of tea-shop or 'dharamshala': something of a lucky dip, since they vary a good deal in comfort and cleanliness.

The trek from Chopta to Tungnath is only three and a half miles, but in that distance one ascends about 3,000 feet, and the pilgrim may be forgiven for feeling that at places he is on a perpendicular path. Like a ladder to heaven, I couldn't help thinking.

In spite of its steepness, my companion, the redoubtable Ganesh Saili, insisted that we take a shortcut. After clawing our way up tufts of alpine grass, which formed the rungs of our ladder, we were stuck and had to inch our way down again; so that the ascent of Tungnath began to resemble a game of Snakes and Ladders.

A tiny guardian-temple dedicated to the god Ganesh spurred us on. Nor was I really fatigued; for the cold fresh air and the verdant greenery surrounding us was like an intoxicant. Myriads of wildflowers grow on the open slopes—buttercups, anemones, wild strawberries, forget-me-not, rock-cress—enough to rival Bhyundar's 'Valley of Flowers' at this time of the year.

But before reaching these alpine meadows, we climb through rhododendron forest, and here one finds at least three species of this flower: the red-flowering tree rhododendron (found throughout the Himalayas between 6,000 feet and 10,000 feet); a second variety, the almatta, with flowers that are light red or rosy in colour; and the third chimul or white variety, found at heights ranging from between 10,000 and 13,000 feet. The chimul is a brush-wood, seldom more than twelve feet high and growing slantingly due to the heavy burden of snow it has to carry for almost six months in the year.

These brushwood rhododendrons are the last trees we see on our ascent, for as we approach Tungnath the tree line ends and there is nothing between earth and sky except grass and rock and tiny flowers. Above us, a couple of crows dive-bomb a hawk, who does his best to escape their attentions. Crows are the world's great survivors. They are capable of living at any height and in any climate; as much at home in the back streets of Delhi as on the heights of Tungnath.

Another survivor up here at any rate, is the pika, a sort of mouse-hare, who looks like neither mouse nor hare but rather a tiny guinea-pig—small ears, no tail, grey-brown fur, and chubby feet. They emerge from their holes under the rocks to forage for grasses on which to feed. Their simple diet and thick fur enable them to live in extreme cold, and they have been found at 16,000 feet, which is higher than where any other mammal lives. The Garhwalis call this little creature the 'runda'—at any rate, that's what the temple priest called it, adding that it was not averse to entering houses and helping itself to grain and other delicacies. So perhaps there's more in it of mouse than of hare.

These little rundas were with us all the way from Chopta to Tungnath; peering out from their rocks or scampering about on the hillside, seemingly unconcerned by our presence. At Tungnath they live beneath the temple flagstones. The priest's grandchildren were having a game discovering their burrows; the rundas would go in at one hole and pop out at another they must have had a system of underground passages.

When we arrived, clouds had gathered over Tungnath, as they do almost every afternoon. The temple looked austere in the gathering gloom.

To some, the name 'rung' indicates 'lofty', from the position of the temple on the highest peak outside the main chain of the Himalayas; others derive it from the word 'tunga', that is 'to be suspended'—an allusion to the form under which the deity is worshipped here. The form is the Swayambhu Ling. On Shivratri or the Night of Shiva, the true believer may, 'with the eye of faith', see the lingam increase in size; but 'to the evil-minded no such favour is granted.'

The temple, though not very large, is certainly impressive, mainly because of its setting and the solid slabs of grey granite from which it is built. The whole place somehow puts me in mind of Emily Bronte's Wuthering Heights—bleak, windswept, open to the skies. And as you look down from the temple at the little half-deserted hamlet that serves it in summer, the eye is met by grey slate roofs and piles of stones, with just a few hardy souls in residence—for the majority of pilgrims now prefer to spend the night down at Chopta.

Even the temple priest, attended by his son and grandsons, complains bitterly of the cold. To spend every day barefoot on those cold flagstones must indeed be hardship. I wince after five minutes of it, made worse by stepping into a puddle of icy water. I shall never make a good pilgrim; no rewards for me, in this world or the next. But the pandit's feet are literally thick-skinned; and the children seem oblivious to the cold. Still in October they must be happy to descend to Maku, their home village on the slopes below Dugalbeta.

It begins to rain as we leave the temple. We pass herds of sheep huddled in a ruined dharamshala. The crows are still rushing about the grey weeping skies, although the hawk has very sensibly gone away. A runda sticks his nose out from his hole, probably to take a look at the weather. There is a clap of thunder and he disappears, like the white rabbit in Alice in Wonderland. We are halfway down the Tungnath 'ladder' when it begins to rain quite heavily. And now we pass our first genuine pilgrims, a group of intrepid Bengalis who are heading straight into the storm. They are without umbrellas or raincoats, but they are not to be deterred. Oaks and rhododendrons flash past as we dash down the steep, winding path. Another short cut, and Ganesh Saili takes a tumble, but is cushioned by moss and buttercups. My wrist-watch strikes a rock and the glass is shattered. No matter. Time here is of little or no consequence. Away with time! Is this, I wonder, the 'bounding and exalting cheerfulness' experienced by Batten and now manifesting itself in me?

The tea-shop beckons. How would one manage in the hills without these wayside tea-shops? Miniature inns, they provide food, shelter and even lodging to dozens at a time. We sit on a bench between a Gujjar herdsman and a pilgrim who is too feverish to make the climb to the temple. He accepts my offer of an aspirin to go with his tea. We tackle some buns-rock-hard, to match our environment—and wash the pellets down with hot sweet tea.

There is a small shrine here too, right in front of the tea-shop. It is a slab of rock roughly shaped like a lingam, and it is daubed with vermilion and strewn with offerings of wildflowers. The mica in the rock gives it a beautiful sheen.

I suppose Hinduism comes closest to being a nature religion. Rivers, rocks, trees, plants, animals and birds, all play their part, both in mythology and in everyday worship.

This harmony is most evident in these remote places, where gods and mountains coexist. Tungnath, as yet unspoilt by a materialistic society, exerts its magic on all who come here with open mind and heart.

Wilson's Bridge

The old wooden bridge has gone, and today an iron suspension bridge straddles the Bhagirathi as it rushes down the gorge below Gangotri. But villagers will tell you that you can still hear the hooves of Wilson's horse as he gallops across the bridge he had built 150 years ago. The legend of Wilson and his pretty hill bride, Gulabi, is still well known in this region.

I had joined some friends in the old forest rest house near the river. There were the Rays, recently married, and the Duttas, married many years. The younger Rays quarrelled frequently; the older Duttas looked on with more amusement than concern. I was a part of their group and yet something of an outsider. As a single man, I was a person of no importance. And as a marriage counsellor, I wouldn't have been of any use to them.

I spent most of my time wandering along the river banks or exploring the thick deodar and oak forests that covered the slopes. It was these trees that had made a fortune for Wilson and his patron, the Raja of Tehri. They had exploited the great forests to the full, floating huge logs downstream to the timber yards in the plains.

Returning to the rest house late one evening, I was halfway across the bridge when I saw a figure at the other end, emerging from the mist. Presently I made out a woman, wearing the plain dhoti of the hills; her hair fell loose over her shoulders. She appeared not to see me, and reclined against the railing of the bridge, looking down at the rushing waters far below. And then, to my amazement and horror, she climbed over the railing and threw herself into the river.

I ran forward, calling out, but I reached the railing only to see her fall into the foaming waters below, from where she was carried swiftly downstream.

The watchman's cabin stood a little way off. The door was open. The watchman, Ram Singh, was reclining on his bed, smoking a hookah.

'Someone just jumped off the bridge,' I said breathlessly. 'She's been swept down the river!'

The watchman was unperturbed. 'Gulabi again,' he said, almost to himself; and then to me, 'Did you see her clearly?'

'Yes, a woman with long loose hair—but I didn't see her face very clearly.'

'It must have been Gulabi. Only a ghost, my dear sir. Nothing to be alarmed about. Every now and then someone sees her throw herself into the river. Sit down,' he said, gesturing towards a battered old armchair, 'be comfortable and I'll tell you all about it.'

I was far from comfortable, but I listened to Ram Singh tell me the tale of Gulabi's suicide. After making me a glass of hot sweet tea, he launched into a long, rambling account of how Wilson, a British adventurer seeking his fortune, had been hunting musk deer when he encountered Gulabi on the path from her village. The girl's grey-green eyes and peach-blossom complexion enchanted him, and he went out of his way to get to know her people. Was he in love with her, or did he simply find her beautiful and desirable? We shall never really know. In the course of his travels and adventures he had known many women, but Gulabi was different, childlike and ingenuous, and he decided he would marry her. The humble family to which she belonged had no objection. Hunting had its limitations, and Wilson found it more profitable to tap the region's great forest wealth. In a few years, he had made a fortune. He built a large timbered house at Harsil, another in Dehradun and a third at Mussoorie. Gulabi had all she could have wanted, including two robust little sons. When he was away on work, she looked after their children and their large apple orchard at Harsil.

And then came the evil day when Wilson met the Englishwoman, Ruth, on the Mussoorie Mall, and decided that she should have a share of his affections and his wealth. A fine house was provided for her, too. The time he spent at Harsil with Gulabi and his children dwindled. 'Business affairs'—he was now one of the owners of a bank—kept him in the fashionable hill resort. He was a popular host and took his friends and associates on shikar parties in the Doon.

Gulabi brought up her children in village style. She heard stories of Wilson's dalliance with the Mussoorie woman and, on one of his rare visits, she confronted him and voiced her resentment, demanding that he leave the other woman. He brushed her aside and told her not to listen to idle gossip. When he turned away from her, she picked up the flintlock pistol that lay on the gun table and fired one shot at him. The bullet missed him and shattered her looking glass. Gulabi ran out of the house, through the orchard and into the forest, then down the steep path to the bridge built by Wilson only two or three years before. When he had recovered his composure, he mounted his horse and came looking for her. It was too late. She had already thrown herself off the bridge into the swirling waters far below. Her body was found a mile or two downstream, caught between some rocks.

This was the tale that Ram Singh told me, with various flourishes and interpolations of his own. I thought it would make a good story to tell my friends that evening, before the fireside in the rest house. They found the story fascinating, but when I told them I had seen Gulabi's ghost, they thought I was doing a little embroidering of my own. Mrs Dutta thought it was a tragic tale. Young Mrs Ray thought Gulabi had been very silly. 'She was a simple girl,' opined Mr Dutta. 'She responded in the only way she knew...'; 'Money can't buy happiness,' said Mr Ray. 'No,' said Mrs Dutta, 'but it can buy you a great many comforts.' Mrs Ray wanted to talk of other things, so I changed the subject. It can get a little confusing for a bachelor who must spend the evening with two married couples. There are undercurrents which he is aware of but not equipped to deal with.

I would walk across the bridge quite often after that. It was busy with traffic during the day, but after dusk there were only a few vehicles on the road and seldom any pedestrians. A mist rose from the gorge below and obscured the far end of the bridge. I preferred walking there in the evening, half expecting, half hoping to see Gulabi's ghost again. It was her face that I really wanted to see. Would she still be as beautiful as she was fabled to be?

It was on the evening before our departure that something happened that would haunt me for a long time afterwards.

There was a feeling of restiveness as our days there drew to a close. The Rays had apparently made up their differences, although they weren't talking very much. Mr Dutta was anxious to get back to his office in Delhi and Mrs Dutta's rheumatism was playing up. I was restless too, wanting to return to my writing desk in Mussoorie.

That evening I decided to take one last stroll across the bridge to enjoy the cool breeze of a summer's night in the mountains. The moon hadn't come up, and it was really quite dark, although there were lamps at either end of the bridge providing sufficient light for those who wished to cross over.

I was standing in the middle of the bridge, in the darkest part, listening to the river thundering down the gorge, when I saw the sari-draped figure emerging from the lamplight and making towards the railings.

Instinctively I called out, 'Gulabi!'

She half turned towards me, but I could not see her clearly. The wind had blown her hair across her face and all I saw was wildly staring eyes. She raised herself over the railing and threw herself off the bridge. I heard the splash as her body struck the water far below.

Once again I found myself running towards the part of the railing where she had jumped. And then someone was running towards the same spot, from the direction of the rest house. It was young Mr Ray.

'My wife!' he cried out. 'Did you see my wife?'

He rushed to the railing and stared down at the swirling waters of the river.

'Look! There she is!' He pointed at a helpless figure bobbing about in the water.

We ran down the steep bank to the river but the current had swept her on. Scrambling over rocks and bushes, we made frantic efforts to catch up with the drowning woman. But the river in that defile is a roaring torrent, and it was over an hour before we were able to retrieve poor Mrs Ray's body, caught in driftwood about a mile downstream.

She was cremated not far from where we found her and we returned to our various homes in gloom and grief, chastened but none the wiser for the experience.

If you happen to be in that area and decide to cross the bridge late in the evening, you might see Gulabi's ghost or hear the hoofbeats of Wilson's horse as he canters across the old wooden bridge looking for her. Or you might see the ghost of Mrs Ray and hear her husband's anguished cry. Or there might be others. Who knows?

A Walk through Garhwal

I wake to what sounds like the din of a factory buzzer, but is in fact the music of a single vociferous cicada in the lime tree near my window.

Through the open window, I focus on a pattern of small, glossy lime leaves; then through them I see the mountains, the Himalayas, striding away into an immensity of sky.

'In a thousand ages of the gods I could not tell thee of the glories of Himachal.' So confessed a Sanskrit poet at the dawn of Indian history and he came closer than anyone else to capturing the spell of the Himalayas. The sea has had Conrad and Stevenson and Masefield, but the mountains continue to defy the written word. We have climbed their highest peaks and crossed their most difficult passes, but still they keep their secrets and their reserve; they remain remote, mysterious, spirit-haunted.

No wonder then, that the people who live on the mountain slopes in the mist-filled valleys of Garhwal, have long since learned humility, patience and a quiet resignation. Deep in the crouching mist lie their villages, while climbing the mountain slopes are forests of rhododendron, spruce and deodar, soughing in the wind from the ice-bound passes. Pale women plough, they laugh at the thunder as their men go down to the plains for work; for little grows on the beautiful mountains in the north wind.

When I think of Manjari village in Garhwal I see a small river, a tributary of the Ganga, rushing along the bottom of a steep, rocky valley. On the banks of the river and on the terraced hills above, there are small fields of corn, barley, mustard, potatoes and onions. A few fruit trees grow near the village. Some hillsides are rugged and bare, just masses of quartz or granite. On hills exposed to wind, only grass and small shrubs are able to obtain a foothold.

This landscape is typical of Garhwal, one of India's most northerly regions with its massive snow ranges bordering on Tibet. Although thinly populated, it does not provide much of a living for its people. Most Garliwali cultivators are poor, some are very poor. 'You have beautiful scenery,' I observed after crossing the first range of hills.

'Yes,' said my friend, 'but we cannot eat the scenery.'

And yet these are cheerful people, sturdy and with wonderful powers of endurance. Somehow they manage to wrest a precarious living from the unhelpful, calcinated soil. I am their guest for a few days.

My friend Gajadhar has brought me to his home, to his village above the little Nayar river. We took a train into the foothills and then we took a bus and finally, made dizzy by the hairpin bends devised in the last century by a brilliantly diabolical road-engineer, we alighted at the small hill station of

Lansdowne, chief recruiting centre for the Garhwal Regiment.

Lansdowne is just over six thousand feet high. From there we walked, covering twenty-five miles between sunrise and sunset, until we came to Manjari village, clinging to the terraced slopes of a very proud, very permanent mountain.

And this is my fourth morning in the village.

Other mornings I was woken by the throaty chuckles of the red-billed blue magpies, as they glided between oak trees and medlars; but today the cicada has drowned all bird song. It is a little out of season for cicadas but perhaps this sudden warm spell in late September has deceived him into thinking it is mating season again.

Early though it is, I am the last to get up. Gajadhar is exercising in the courtyard, going through an odd combination of Swedish exercises and yoga. He has a fine physique with the sturdy legs that most Garhwalis possess. I am sure he will realize his ambition of joining the Indian Army as a cadet. His younger brother Chakradhar, who is slim and fair with high cheek-bones, is milking the family's buffalo. Normally, he would be on his long walk to school, five miles distant; but this is a holiday, so he can stay at home and help with the household chores.

His mother is lighting a fire. She is a handsome woman even though her ears, weighed clown by heavy silver earrings have lost their natural shape. Garhwali women usually invest their savings in silver ornaments. And at the time of marriage it is the boy's parents who make a gift of land to the parents of an attractive girl; a dowry system in reverse. There are fewer women than men in the hills and their good looks and sturdy physique give them considerable status among the men-folk.

Chakradhar's father is a corporal in the Indian Army and is away for most of the year.

When Gajadhar marries, his wife will stay in the village to help his mother and younger brother look after the fields, house, goats and buffalo. Gajadhar will see her only when he comes home on leave. He prefers it that way; he does not think a simple hill girl should be exposed to the sophisticated temptations of the plains.

The village is far above the river and most of the fields depend on rainfall. But water must be fetched for cooking, washing and drinking. And so, after a breakfast of hot sweet milk and thick *chajmaues* stuffed with minced radish, the brothers and I set off down the rough track to the river.

The still has climbed the mountains but it has yet to reach the narrow valley. We bathe in the river, Gjadhar and Chakradhar dive off a massive rock; but I wade in circumspectly, unfamiliar with the river's depths and currents. The water, a milky blue has come from the melting snows; it is very cold. I bathe quickly and then dash for a strip of sand where a little sunshine has split down the mountainside in warm, golden pools of light. At the same time the song of the whistling-thrush emerges like a dark secret from the wooded shadows. A little later, buckets filled we toil up the steep mountain. We must go by a better path this time if we are not to come tumbling down with our buckets of water. As we climb we are mocked by it barbet which sits high up in a spruce calling feverishly in its monotonous mournful way.

'We call it the mewli bird,' says Gajadhar, 'there is a story about it. People say that the souls of men who have suffered

injuries in the law courts of the plains and who have died of
their disappointments, transmigrate into the mewli birds. That
is why the birds are always crying *un, raee-oru, un nee ow,* which
means "injustice, injustice!"'

The path leads us past a primary school, a small temple,
and a single shop in which it is possible to buy salt, soap and
a few other necessities. It is also the post office. And today it
is serving as a lock-up.

The villagers have apprehended a local thief, who specializes
in stealing jewellery from women while they are working in the
fields. He is awaiting escort to the Lansdowne police station,
and the shop-keeper-cum-postmaster-cum-constable brings him
out for us to inspect. He is a mild-looking fellow, clearly shy of
the small crowd that has gathered round him. I wonder how he
manages to deprive the strong hill-women of their jewellery;
it could not be by force! Any cases of crimes and violence are
rare in Garhwal; and robbery too, is uncommon for the simple
reason that there is very little to rob.

The thief is rather glad of my presence, as it distracts
attention from him. Strangers seldom come to Manjari. The
crowd leaves him, turns to me, eager to catch a glimpse of the
stranger in its midst. The children exclaim, point at me with
delight, chatter among themselves. I might be a visitor from
another planet instead of just an itinerant writer from the plains.

The postman has yet to arrive. The mail is brought in relays
from Lansdowne. The Manjari postman who has to cover eight
miles and delivers letters at several small villages on his route,
should arrive around noon. He also serves as a newspaper,
bringing the villagers news of the outside world. Over the

years he has acquired a reputation for being highly inventive, sometimes creating his own news; so much so that when he told the villagers that men had landed on the moon, no one believed him. There are still a few sceptics.

Gajadhar has been walking out of the village every day, anxious to meet the postman. He is expecting a letter giving the results of his army entrance examination. If he is successful he will be called for an interview. And then, if he is accepted, he will be trained as an officer-cadet. After two years he will become a second lieutenant. His father, after twelve years in the army is still only a corporal. But his father never went to school. There were no schools in the hills during his father's youth.

The Manjari school is only up to class five and it has about forty pupils. If these children (most of them boys) want to study any further, then, like Chakradhar, they must walk the five miles to the high school at the next big village.

'Don't you get tired walking ten miles every day?' I ask Chakradhar.

'I am used to it,' he says. 'I like walking.'

I know that he only has two meals a day—one at seven in the morning when he leaves home and the other at six or seven in the evening when he returns from school—and I ask him if he does not get hungry on the way.

'There is always the wild fruit,' he replies.

It appears that he is an expert on wild fruit: the purple berries of the thorny bilberry bushes ripening in May and June; wild strawberries like drops of blood on the dark green monsoon grass; small sour cherries and tough medlars in the winter months. Chakradhai's strong teeth and probing tongue extract whatever

tang or sweetness lies hidden in them. And in March there are
the rhododendron flowers. His mother makes them into jam.
But Chakradhar likes them as they are: he places the petals on
his tongue and chews till the sweet juice trickles down his throat.

He has never been ill.

'But what happens when someone is ill?' I ask knowing that
in Manjari there are no medicines, no dispensary or hospital.

'He goes to bed until he is better,' says Gajadhar. 'We
have a few home remedies. But if someone is very sick, we
carry the person to the hospital at Lansdowne.' He pauses as
though wondering how much he should say, then shrugs and
says: 'Last year my uncle was very ill. He had a terrible pain
in his stomach. For two days he cried out with the pain. So we
made a litter and started out for Lansdowne. We had already
carried him fifteen miles when he died. And then we had to
carry him back again.'

Some of the villages have dispensaries managed by
compounders but the remoter areas of Garhwal are completely
without medical aid. To the outsider, life in the Garhwal hills
may seem idyllic and the people simple. But the Garhwali is far
from being simple and his life is one long struggle, especially if
he happens to be living in a high altitude village snowbound for
four months in the year, with cultivation coming to a standstill
and people having to manage with the food gathered and stored
during the summer months.

Fortunately, the clear mountain air and the simple diet keep
the Garhwalis free from most diseases, and help them recover
from the more common ailments. The greatest dangers come
from unexpected disasters, such as an accident with an axe

or scythe, or an attack by a wild animal. A few years back, several Manjari children and old women were killed by a man-eating leopard. The leopard was finally killed by the villagers who hunted it down with spears and axes. But the leopard that sometimes prowls round the village at night looking for a stray dog or goat, slinks away at the approach of a human.

I do not see the leopard but at night I am woken by a rumbling and thumping on the roof. I wake Gajadhar and ask him what is happening.

'It is only a bear,' he says.

'Is it trying to get in?'

'No, it's been in the cornfield and now it's after the pumpkins on the roof.'

A little later, when we look out of the small window, we see a black bear making off like a thief in the night, a large pumpkin held securely to his chest.

At the approach of winter when snow covers the higher mountains, the brown and black Himalayan bears descend to lower altitudes in search of food. Because they are short-sighted and suspicious of anything that moves, they can be dangerous; but, like most wild animals, they will avoid men if they can and are aggressive only when accompanied by their cubs.

Gajadhar advises me to run downhill if chased by a bear. He says that bears find it easier to run uphill than downhill.

I am not interested in being chased by a bear, but the following night Gajadhar and I stay up to try and prevent the bear from depleting his cornfield. We take up our position on a highway promontory of rock, which gives us a clear view of the moonlit field.

A little after midnight, the bear comes down to the edge of the field but he is suspicious and has probably smelt us. He is, however, hungry; and so, after standing up as high as possible on his hind legs and peering about to see if the field is empty, he comes cautiously out of the forest and makes his way towards the corn.

When about half-way, his attention is suddenly attracted by some Buddhist prayer-flags which have been strung up recently between two small trees by a band of wandering Tibetans. On spotting the flags the bear gives a little grunt of disapproval and begins to move back into the forest; but the fluttering of the little flags is a puzzle that he feels he must make out (for a bear is one of the most inquisitive animals); so after a few backward steps, he again stops and watches them.

Not satisfied with this, he stands on his hind legs looking at the flags, first at one side and then at the other. Then seeing that they do not attack him and so not appear dangerous, he makes his way right up to the flags taking only two or three steps at it dine and having a good look before each advance. Eventually, he moves confidently up to the flags and pulls them all down. Then, after careful examination of the flags, he moves into the field of corn.

But Gajadhar has decided that he is not going to lose any more corn, so he starts shouting, and the rest of the village wakes up and people come out of their houses beating drums and empty kerosene tins.

Deprived of his dinner, the bear makes off in a bad temper. He runs downhill and at a good speed too; and I am glad that I am not in his path just then. Uphill or downhill, an angry bear is best given a very wide berth.

For Gajadhar, impatient to know the result of his array entrance examination, the following day is a trial of his patience.

First, we hear that there has been a landslide and that the postman cannot reach us. Then, we hear that although there has been a landslide, the postman has already passed the spot in safety. Another alarming rumour has it that the postman disappeared with the landslide. This is soon denied. The postman is safe. It was only the mail-bag that disappeared.

And then, at two in the afternoon, the postman turns up. He tells us that there was indeed a landslide but that it took place on someone else's route. Apparently, a mischievous urchin who passed him on the way was responsible for all the rumours. But we suspect the postman of having something to do with them...

Gajadhar had passed his examination and will leave with me in the morning. We have to be up early in order to reach Lansdowne before dark. But Gajadhar's mother insists on celebrating her son's success by feasting her friends and neighbours. There is a partridge (a present from a neighbour who had decided that Gajadhar will make a fine husband for his daughter), and two chickens: rich fare for folk whose normal diet consists mostly of lentils, potatoes and onions.

After dinner, there are songs, and Gajadhar's mother sings of the homesickness of those who are separated from their loved ones and their home in the hills. It is an old Garhwali folk-song:

Oh, mountain-swift, you are from my father's home;
Speak, oh speak, in the courtyard of my parents,
My mother will hear you; She will send my brother to fetch me.

A grain of rice alone in the cooking pot
Cries, 'I wish I could get out!'
Likewise I wonder:
'Will I ever reach my father's house?'

The hookah is passed round and stories are told. Tales of ghosts and demons mingle with legends of ancient kings and heroes. It is almost midnight by the time the last guest has gone. Chakradhar approaches me as I am about to retire for the night.

'Will you come again?' he asks.

'Yes, I'll come again,' I reply. 'If not next year, then the year after. How many years are left before you finish school?'

'Four'.

'Four years. If you walk ten miles a day for four years, how many miles will that make?'

'Four thousand and six hundred miles,' says Chakradhar after a moment's thought, 'but we have two months' holiday each year. That means I'll walk about twelve thousand miles in four years.'

The moon has not yet risen. Lanterns swing in the dark.

The lanterns flit silently over the hillside and go out one by one. This Garhwali day, which is just like any other day in the hills, slips quietly into the silence of the mountains.

I stretch myself out on my cot. Outside the small window the sky is brilliant with stars. As I close my eyes, someone brushes against the lime tree, brushing its leaves; and the fresh fragrance of lines comes to me on the night air, making the moment memorable for all time.

Cold Beer at Chutmalpur

Just outside the small market town of Chutmalpur (on the way back from Delhi) one is greeted by a large signboard with just two words on it: Cold Beer. The signboard is almost as large as the shop from which the cold beer is dispensed; but after a gruelling five-hour drive from Delhi, in the heat and dust of May, a glass of chilled beer is welcome—except, of course, to teetotallers who will find other fizzy ways to satiate their thirst.

Chutmalpur is not the sort of place you'd choose to retire in. But it has its charms, not the least of which is its Sunday Market, when the varied produce of the rural interior finds its way on to the dusty pavements, and the air vibrates with noise, colour and odours. Carpets of red chillies, seasonal fruits, stacks of grain and vegetables, cheap toys for the children, bangles of lac, wooden artifacts, colourful underwear, sweets of every description, *churan* to go with them...

'*Lakar hajam, gather hajam!*' cries the churan-seller. Translated: Digest wood, digest stones! That is, if you partake of this particular digestive pill which, when I tried it, appeared to be one part hing (asafoetida) and one part gunpowder. Things are seldom what they seem to be. Passing through the small town of Purkazi, I noticed a sign-board which announced the availability of 'Books'—just that. Intrigued, I stopped to find out more about this bookshop in the wilderness. Perhaps I'd find a rare tome to add to my library. Peeping in, I discovered that the dark interior was stacked from floor to ceiling with exercise books! Apparently the shop-owner was the supplier for the district.

Rare books can be seen in Roorkee, in the University's old library. Here, not many years ago, a First Folio Shakespeare turned up and was celebrated in the Indian Press as a priceless discovery. Perhaps it's still there.

Also in the library is a bust of Sir Proby Cautley, who conceived and built the Ganga Canal, which starts at Haridwar and passes through Roorkee on its way across the Doab. Hardly anyone today has heard of Cautley, and yet surely his achievement outstrips that of many Englishmen in India— soldiers and statesmen who became famous for doing all the wrong things.

Cautley's Canal

Cautley came to India at the age of seventeen and joined the Bengal Artillery. In 1825, he assisted Captain Robert Smith, the engineer in charge of constructing the Eastern Yamuna Canal. By 1836 he was Superintendent-General of Canals. From the start, he worked towards his dream of building a Ganga Canal, and spent six months walking and riding through the jungles and countryside, taking each level and measurement himself, sitting up all night to transfer them to his maps. He was confident that a 500-kilometre canal was feasible. There were many objections and obstacles to his project, most of them financial, but Cautley persevered and eventually persuaded the East India Company to back him.

Digging of the canal began in 1839. Cautley had to make his own bricks—millions of them—his own brick kiln, and his own mortar. A hundred thousand tonnes of lime went into the mortar, the other main ingredient of which was *surkhi*, made by grinding over-burnt bricks to a powder. To reinforce the mortar, *ghur*, ground lentils and jute fibres were added to it.

Initially, opposition came from the priests in Haridwar, who felt that the waters of the holy Ganga would be imprisoned. Cautley pacified them by agreeing to leave a narrow gap in the dam through which the river water could flow unchecked. He won over the priests when he inaugurated his project with aarti, and the worship of Ganesh, God of Good Beginnings. He also undertook the repair of the sacred bathing ghats along the river. The canal banks were also to have their own ghats with steps leading down to the water.

The headworks of the canal are at Haridwar, where the Ganga enters the plains after completing its majestic journey through the Himalayas. Below Haridwar, Cautley had to dig new courses for some of the mountain torrents that threatened the canal. He collected them into four steams and took them over the canal by means of four passages. Near Roorkee, the land fell away sharply and here Cautley had to build an aqueduct, a masonry bridge that carries the canal for half a kilometre across the Solani torrent—a unique engineering feat. At Roorkee, the canal is twenty-five metres higher than the parent river which flows almost parallel to it.

Most of the excavation work on the canal was done mainly by the Oads, a gypsy tribe who were professional diggers for most of northwest India. They took great pride in their work. Though extremely poor, Cautley found them a happy and carefree lot who worked in a very organized manner.

When the canal was formally opened on the 8 April 1854, its main channel was 348 miles long, its branches 306 and the distributaries over 3,000. Over 7,67,000 acres in 5,000 villages were irrigated. One of its main branches re-entered the Ganga at Kanpur; it also had branches to Fatehgarh, Bulandshahr and Aligarh.

Cautley's achievements did not end there. He was also actively involved in Dr Falconer's fossil expedition in the Siwaliks. He presented to the British Museum an extensive collection of fossil mammalia—including hippopotamus and crocodile fossils, evidence that the region was once swampland or an inland sea. Other animal remains found here included the sabre-toothed tiger; Elephis ganesa, an elephant with a trunk ten-and-a-half feet long; a three-toed ancestor of the horse; the bones of a fossil ostrich; and the remains of giant cranes and tortoises. Exciting times, exciting finds.

Nor did Cautley's interests and activities end in fossil excavation. My copy of Surgeon General Balfour's Cyclopedia of India (1873) lists a number of fascinating reports and papers by Cautley. He wrote on a submerged city, twenty feet underground, near Behut in the Doab; on the coal and lignite in the Himalayas; on gold washings in the Siwalik Hills, between the Jamuna and Sutlej rivers; on a new species of snake; on the mastodons of the Siwaliks; on the manufacture of tar; and on Panchukkis or corn mills.

How did he find time for all this, I wonder. Most of his life was spent in tents, overseeing the canal work or digging up fossils. He had a house in Mussoorie (one of the first), but he could not have spent much time in it. It is today part of the Manav Bharti School, and there is still a plaque in the office stating that Cautley lived there. Perhaps he wrote some of his reports and expositions during brief sojourns in the hills. It is said that his wife left him, unable to compete against the rival attractions of canals and fossils remains.

I wonder, too, if there was any follow up on his reports of the submerged city—is it still there, waiting to be re-discovered— or his findings on gold washings in the Siwaliks. Should my royalties ever dry up, I might just wonder off into the Siwaliks, looking for 'gold in them that hills'. Meanwhile, whenever I travel by road from Delhi to Haridwar, and pass over that placid canal at various places en-route, I think of the man who spent more than twenty years of his life in executing this magnificent project, and others equally demanding. And then, his work done, walking away from it all without thought of fame or fortune.

A Jungle Princess

From Roorkee separate roads lead to Haridwar, Saharanpur, Dehradun. And from the Saharanpur road you can branch off to Paonta Sahib, with its famous gurudwara glistening above the blue waters of the Yamuna. Still blue up here, but not so blue by the time it enters Delhi. Industrial affluents and human waste soon muddy the purest of rivers.

From Paonta you can turn right to Herbertpur, a small township originally settled by an Anglo-Indian family early in the nineteenth century. As may be inferred by its name, Herbert was the scion of the family, but I have been unable to discover much about him. When I was a boy, the Carberry family owned much of the land around here, but by the time Independence came, only one of the family remained—Doreen, a sultry, dusky beauty who become known in Dehra as the 'Jungle Princess'. Her husband had deserted her, but she had a small daughter who grew up on the land. Doreen's income came from her mango and guava orchards, and she seemed quite happy living in this isolated rural area near the river. Occasionally she came into Dehra Dun, a bus ride of a couple of hours, and she would visit my mother, a childhood friend, and occasionally stay overnight.

On one occasion we went to Doreen's jungle home for a couple of days. I was just seven or eight years old. I remember Doreen's daughter (about my age) teaching me to climb trees. I managed the guava tree quite well, but some of the others were too difficult for me.

How did this jungle queen manage to live by herself in this remote area, where her house, orchard and fields were bordered by forest on one side and the river on the other?

Well, she had her servants of course, and they were loyal to her. And she also possessed several guns, and could handle them very well. I saw her bring down a couple of pheasants with her twelve-bore spread shot. She had also killed a cattle-lifting tiger which had been troubling a nearby village, and a marauding leopard that had taken one of her dogs. So she was quite capable of taking care of herself. When I last saw her, some twenty-five years ago, she was in her seventies. I believe she sold her land and went to live elsewhere with her daughter, who by then had a family of her own.

From the Pool to the Glacier

1
My Boyhood Pool

It was going to rain. I could see the rain moving across the foothills, and I could smell it on the breeze. But instead of turning homewards I pushed my way through the leaves and brambles that grew across the forest path. I had heard the sound of running water at the bottom of the hill, and I was determined to find this hidden stream.

I had to slide down a rock-face into a small ravine and there I found the stream running over a bed of shingle, I removed my shoes and started walking upstream. A large glossy black bird with a curved red beak hooted at me as I passed; and a Paradise Flycatcher—this one I couldn't fail to recognize, with its long fan-tail beating the air-swooped across the stream. Water trickled down from the hillside, from amongst ferns and grasses and wild flowers; and the hills, rising steeply on either side, kept the ravine in shadow. The rocks were smooth, almost soft, and some of them were gray and some yellow. A small waterfall came down the rocks and formed a deep round pool of apple-green water.

When I saw the pool I turned and ran home. I wanted to tell Anil and Kamal about it. It began to rain, but I didn't stop to take shelter, I ran all the way home—through the *sal* forest, across the dry river-bed through the outskirts of the town.

Though Anil usually chose the adventures we were to have, the pool was my own discovery, and I was proud of it.

'We'll call it Rusty's Pool,' said Kamal. 'And remember, it's a secret pool. No one else must know of it.'

I think it was the pool that brought us together more than anything else.

Kamal was the best swimmer. He dived off rocks and went gliding about under the water like a long golden fish. Anil had strong legs and arms, and he threshed about with much vigour but little skill. I could dive off a rock too, but I usually landed on my stomach.

There were slim silver fish in the stream. At first we tried catching them with a line, but they soon learnt the art of taking the bait without being caught on the hook. Next, we tried a bedsheet (Anil had removed it from his mother's laundry) which we stretched across one end of the stream; but the fish wouldn't come anywhere near it. Eventually, Anil without telling us, procured a stick of gunpowder. And Kamal and I were startled out of an afternoon siesta by a flash across the water and a deafening explosion. Half the hillside tumbled into the pool, and Anil along with it. We got him out, along with a large supply of stunned fish which were too small for eating. Anil, however, didn't want all his work to go to waste; so he roasted the fish over a fire and ate them himself.

The effects of the explosion gave Anil another idea, which was to enlarge our pool by building a dam across one end. This he accomplished with our combined labour. But he had chosen a week when there had been heavy rain in the hills, and we had barely finished the dam when a torrent of water came rushing down the bed of the stream and burst our earthworks, flooding the ravine. Our clothes were carried away by the current, and we had to wait until it was night before creeping into town through the darkest alley-ways. Anil was spotted at a street corner, but he posed as a naked Sadhu and began calling for alms, and finally slipped in through the back door of his house without being recognized. I had to lend Kamal some of my clothes, and these, being on the small side, made him look odd and gangly. Our other activities at the pool included wrestling and buffalo-riding.

We wrestled on a strip of sand that ran beside the stream. Anil had often attended wrestling akharas and was something of an expert. Kamal and I usually combined against him, and after five or ten minutes of furious unscientific struggle, we usually succeeded in flattening Anil into the sand. Kamal would sit on his head, and I would sit on his legs until he admitted defeat. There was no fun in taking him on singly, because he knew too many tricks for us.

We rode on a couple of buffaloes that sometimes came to drink and wallow in the more muddy parts of the stream. Buffaloes are fine, sluggish creatures, always in search of a soft, slushy resting place. We would climb on their backs, and kick and yell and urge them forward; but on no occasion did we succeed in getting them to carry us anywhere. If they got tired of our antics, they would merely roll over on their backs, taking us with them into a bed of muddy water.

Not that it mattered how muddy we got, because we had only to dive into the pool to get rid of it all. The buffaloes couldn't get to the pool because of its narrow outlet and the slippery rocks.

If it was possible for Anil and me to leave our homes at night, we would come to the pool for a swim by moonlight. We would often find Kamal there before us. He wasn't afraid of the dark or the surrounding forest, where there were panthers and jungle cats. We bathed silently at night, because the stillness of the surrounding jungle seemed to discourage high spirits; but sometimes Kamal would sing—he had a clear, ringing voice—and we would float the red, long-fingered poinsettias downstream.

The pool was to be our principal meeting place during the coming months. It was not that we couldn't meet in town. But the pool was secret, known only to us, and it gave us a feeling of conspiracy and adventure to meet there after school. It was at the pool that we made our plans: it was at the pool that we first spoke of the glacier; but several weeks and a few other exploits were to pass before the particular dream materialized.

2
Ghosts on the Verandah

Anil's mother's memory was stored with an incredible amount of folklore, and she would sometimes astonish us with her stories of spirits and mischievous ghosts.

One evening, when Anil's father was out of town, and Kamal and I had been invited to stay the night at Anil's upper-storey flat in the bazaar, his mother began to tell us about the various types of ghosts she had known. Melia, a servant-girl, having just taken a bath, came out on the verandah, with her hair loose.

'My girl, you ought not to leave your hair loose like that,' said Anil's mother. 'It is better to tie a knot in it.'

'But I have not oiled it yet,' said Mulia.

'Never mind, but you should not leave your hair loose towards sunset. There are spirits called *jinns* who are attracted by long hair and pretty black eyes like yours. They may be tempted to carry you away!'

'How dreadful!' exclaimed Mulia, hurriedly tying a knot in her hair, and going indoors to be on the safe side.

Kamal and I sat on a string cot, facing Anil's mother, who sat on another cot. She was not much older than thirty-two, and had often been mistaken for Anil's elder sister; she came from a village near Mathura, a part of the country famous for its gods and spirits and demons.

'Can you see *jinns*, aunty-ji?' I asked.

'Sometimes,' she said. 'There was an Urdu teacher in Mathura, whose pupils were about the same age as you. One of the boys was very good at his lessons. One day, while he sat at his desk in a corner of the classroom, the teacher asked him to fetch a book from the cupboard which stood at the far end of the room. The boy, who felt lazy that morning, didn't move from his seat. He merely stretched out his hand, took the book from the cupboard, and handed it to the teacher. Everyone was astonished, because the boy's arm had stretched about four yards before touching the book! They realized that he was a *jinn;* that was the reason for his being so good at games and exercises which required great agility.'

'Well, I wish I was a *jinn,*' said Anil. 'Especially for volleyball matches.'

Anil's mother then told us about *Munjia,* a mischievous ghost who lives in lonely peepul trees. When a *Munjia* is annoyed, he rushes out from his tree and upsets tongas, bullock-carts and cycles. Even a bus is known to have been upset by a *Munjia.*

'If you are passing beneath a peepul tree at night,' warned Anil's mother, 'be careful not to yawn without covering your mouth or snapping your fingers in front of it. If you don't remember to do that, the *Munjia* will jump down your throat and completely ruin your digestion!'

In an attempt to change the subject, Kamal mentioned that a friend of his had found a snake in his bed one morning.

'Did he kill it?' asked Anil's mother anxiously.

'No, it slipped away,' said Kamal.

'Good,' she said. 'It is lucky if you see a snake early in the morning.'

'It won't bite you if you let it alone,' she said.

By eleven o'clock, after we had finished our dinner and heard a few more ghost stories—including one about Anil's grandmother, whose spirit paid the family a visit—Kamal and I were most reluctant to leave the company on the verandah and retire to the room which had been set apart for us. It did not make us feel any better to be told by Anil's mother that we should recite certain magical verses to keep away the more mischievous spirits. We tried one, which went—

Bhoot, pret, pisach, dana
Chhoo mantar, sab nikal jana,
Mano, mano, Shiv ka kahna...

which, roughly translated, means—

Ghosts, spirits, goblins, sprites,
Away you fly, don't come tonight,
Or with great Shiva you'll have to fight!

Shiva, the Destroyer, is one of the three major Hindu deities. But the more we repeated the verse, the more uneasy we became, and when I got into bed (after carefully examining it for snakes), I couldn't lie still, but kept twisting and turning and looking at the walls for moving shadows. Kamal attempted to raise our spirits by singing softly, but this only made the atmosphere more eerie. After a while we heard someone knocking at the door, and the voices of Anil and the maidservant. Getting up and opening the door, I found them looking pale and anxious. They, too, had succeeded in frightening themselves as a result of Anil's mother's stories.

'Are you all right?' asked Anil. 'Wouldn't you like to sleep in our part of the house? It might be safer. Melia will help us to carry the beds across!'

'We're quite all right,' protested Kamal and I, refusing to admit we were nervous; but we were hustled along to the other side of the flat as though a band of ghosts was conspiring against us. Anil's mother had been absent during all this activity but suddenly we heard her screaming from the direction of the room we had just left.

'Rusty and Kamal have disappeared!' she cried. 'Their beds have gone, too!'

And then, when she came out on the verandah and saw us clashing about in our pyjamas, she gave another scream and collapsed on a cot.

After that, we didn't allow Anil's mother to tell us ghost stories at night.

3
To the Hills

At the end of August, when the rains were nearly over, we met at the pool to make plans for the autumn holidays. We had bathed, and were stretched out in the shade of the fresh, rain-washed *sal* trees, when Kamal, pointing vaguely to the distant mountains, said: 'Why don't we go to the Pindari Glacier?'

'The glacier!' exclaimed Anil. 'But that's all snow and ice!'

'Of course it is,' said Kamal. 'But there's a path through the mountains that goes all the way to the foot of the glacier. It's only fifty-four miles!'

'Do you mean we must walk fifty-four miles?'

'Well, there's no other way,' said Kamal. 'Unless you prefer to sit on a mine. But your legs are too long, they'll be trailing along the ground. No, we'll have to walk. It will take us about ten days to get to the glacier and back, but if we take enough food there'll be no problem. There are *dak* bungalows to stay in at night.'

'Kamal gets all the best ideas,' I said. 'But I suppose Anil and I will have to get our parents' permission. And some money.'

'My mother won't let me go,' said Anil. 'She says the

mountains are full of ghosts. And she thinks I'll get up to some mischief. How can one get up to mischief on a lonely mountain?'

'I'm sure it won't be dangerous, people are always going to the glacier. Can you see that peak above the others on the right?' Kamal pointed to the distant snow-range, barely visible against the soft blue sky. 'The Pindari Glacier is below it. It's at 12,000 feet, I think, but we won't need any special equipment. There'll be snow only for the final two or three miles. Do you know that it's the beginning of the river Sarayu?'

'You mean our river?' asked Anil, thinking of the little river that wandered along the outskirts of the town, joining the Ganges further downstream.

'Yes. But it's only a trickle where it starts.'

'How much money will we need?' I asked, determined to be practical.

'Well, I've saved twenty rupees,' said Kamal.

'But won't you need that for your books?' I asked.

'No, this is extra. If each of us brings twenty rupees, we should have enough. There's nothing to spend money on, once we are up on the mountains. There are only one or two villages on the way, and food is scarce, so we'll have to take plenty of food with us. I learnt all this from the Tourist Office.'

'Kamal's been planning this without our knowledge,' complained Anil.

'He always plans in advance,' I said, 'but it's a good idea, and it should be a fine adventure.'

'All right,' said Anil. 'But Rusty will have to be with me when I ask my mother. She thinks Rusty is very sensible, and might let me go if he says it's quite safe.' And he ended the discussion by jumping into the pool, where we soon joined him.

Though my mother hesitated about letting me go, my father said it was a wonderful idea, and was only sorry because he couldn't accompany us himself (which was a relief, as we didn't want our parents along); and though Anil's father hesitated—or rather, because he hesitated—his mother said yes, of course Anil must go, the mountain air would be good for his health. A puzzling remark, because Anil's health had never been better. The bazaar people, when they heard that Anil might be away for a couple of weeks, were overjoyed at the prospect of a quiet spell, and pressed his father to let him go.

On a cloudy day, promising rain, we bundled ourselves into the bus that was to take us to Kapkote (where people lose their caps and coats, punned Anil), the starting point of our trek. Each of us carried a haversack, and we had also brought along a good sized bedding-roll which, apart from blankets, also contained rice and flour thoughtfully provided by Anil's mother. We had no idea how we would carry the bedding-roll once we started walking; but an astrologer had told Anil's mother it was a good day for travelling, so we didn't worry much over minor details.

We were soon in the hills, on a winding road that took us up and up, until we saw the valley and our town spread out beneath us, the river a silver ribbon across the plain. Kamal pointed to a patch of dense sal forest and said, 'Our pool must be there!' We took a sharp bend, and the valley disappeared, and the mountains towered above us.

We had dull headaches by the time we reached Kapkote; but when we got down from the bus a cool breeze freshened us.

At the wayside shop we drank glasses of hot sweet tea, and the shopkeeper told us we could spend the night in one of his rooms. It was pleasant at Kapkote, the hills wooded with deodar trees, the lower slopes planted with fresh green paddy. At night, there was a wind moaning in the trees, and it found its way through the cracks in the windows and eventually through our blankets. Then, right outside the door, a dog began howling at the moon. It had been a good day for travelling, but the astrologer hadn't warned us that it would be a bad night for sleep.

Next morning we washed our faces at a small stream about a hundred yards from the shop, and filled our water bottles for the day's march. A boy from the nearby village sat on a rock, studying our movements.

'Where are you going?' he asked, unable to suppress his curiosity.

'To the glacier,' said Kamal.

'Let me come with you,' said the boy. 'I know the way.'

'You're too small,' said Anil. 'We need someone who can carry our bedding-roll.'

'I'm small,' said the boy, 'but I'm strong. I'm not a weakling like the boys in the plains.' Though he was shorter than any of us, he certainly looked sturdy, and had a muscular well-knit body and pink cheeks. 'See!' he said; and picking up a rock the size of a football, he heaved it across the stream.

'I think he can come with us,' I said.

And the boy, whose name was Bisnu, clashed off to inform his people of his employment—we had agreed to pay him a rupee a day for acting as our guide and 'sherpa'.

And then we were walking—at first, above the little Sarayu

river, then climbing higher along the rough mule track, always within sound of the water. Kamal wanted to bathe in the river. I said it was too far, and Anil said we wouldn't reach the dak bungalow before dark if we went for a swim. Regretfully, we left the river behind, and marched on through a forest of oaks, over wet, rotting leaves that made a soft carpet for our feet. We ate at noon, under an oak. As we didn't want to waste any time making a fire—not on this first crucial day—we ate beans from a tin and drank most of our water.

In the afternoon, we came to the river again. The water was swifter now, green and bubbling, still far below us. We saw two boys—in the water, swimming in an inlet which reminded us of our own secret pool. They waved, and invited us to join them. We returned their greeting; but it would have taken us an hour to get down to the river and up again; so we continued on our way.

We walked fifteen miles on the first day—our speed was to decrease after this—and we were at the dak bungalow by six o'clock. Bisnu busied himself collecting sticks for a fire. Anil found the bungalow's watchman asleep in a patch of fading sunlight, and roused him. The watchman, who hadn't been bothered by visitors for weeks, grumbled at our intrusion, but opened a room for us. He also produced some potatoes from his quarters, and these were roasted for dinner.

It became cold after the sun had gone down, and we remained close to Bisnu's fire. The damp sticks burnt fitfully. But Bisnu had justified his inclusion in our party. He had balanced the bedding-roll on his shoulders as though it were full of cotton wool instead of blankets. Now he was helping with the cooking.

And we were glad to have him sharing our hot potatoes and strong tea.

There were only two beds in the room, and we pushed these together, apportioning out the blankets as fairly as possible. Then the four of us leapt into bed, shivering in the cold. We were already over 5,000 feet. Bisnu, in his own peculiar way, had wrapped a scarf round his neck, though a cotton singlet and shorts were all that he wore for the night.

'Tell us a story, Rusty,' said Anil. 'It will help us to fall asleep.'

I told them one of his mother's stories, about a boy and a girl who had been changed into a pair of buffaloes; and then Bisnu told us about the ghost of a Sadhu, who was to be seen sitting in the snow by moonlight, not far from the glacier. Far from putting us to sleep, this story kept us awake for hours.

'Aren't you asleep yet?' I asked Anil in the middle of the night.

'No, you keep kicking me,' he lied.

'We don't have enough blankets,' complained Kamal, 'It's too cold to sleep.'

'I never sleep till it's very late,' mumbled Bisnu from the bottom of the bed.

No one was prepared to admit that our imaginations were keeping us awake.

After a little while we heard a thud on the corrugated tin sheeting, and then the sound of someone—or something— scrambling about on the roof. Anil, Kamal and I sat up in bed, startled out of our wits. Bisnu, who had been winning the race to be fast asleep, merely turned over on his side and grunted.

'It's only a bear,' he said. 'Didn't you notice the pumpkins on the roof? Bears love pumpkins.'

For half an hour we had to listen to the bear as it clambered about on the roof, feasting on the watchman's ripening pumpkins. Finally, there was silence. Kamal and I crawled out of our blankets and went to the window. And through the frosted glass we saw a black Himalayan bear ambling across the slope in front of the bungalow, a fat pumpkin held between its paws.

4

To The River

It was raining when we woke, and the mountains were obscured by a heavy mist. We delayed our departure, playing football on the verandah with one of the pumpkins that had fallen off the roof. At noon the rain stopped, and the sun shone through the clouds. As the mist lifted, we saw the snow range, the great peaks of Nanda Kot and Trisul stepping into the sky.

'It's different up here,' said Kamal. 'I feel a different person.

'That's the altitude,' I said. 'As we go higher, we'll get lighter in the head.'

'Anil is light in the head already,' said Kamal. 'I hope the altitude isn't too much for him.'

'If you two are going to be witty,' said Anil, 'I shall go off with Bisnu, and you'll have to find the way yourselves.'

Bisnu grinned at each of us in turn to show us that he wasn't taking sides; and after a breakfast of boiled eggs, we set off on our trek to the next bungalow.

Rain had made the ground slippery, and we were soon ankle-deep in slush. Our next bungalow lay in a narrow valley, on the banks of the rushing Pindar river, which twisted its way through the mountains. We were not sure how far we had to go, but nobody seemed in a hurry. On an impulse, I decided to hurry on ahead of the others. I wanted to be waiting for them at the river.

When Anil, Kamal and Bisnu arrived, the four of us bravely decided to bathe in the little river. The late afternoon sun was still warm, but the water—so clear and inviting—proved to be ice-cold. Only twenty miles upstream the river emerged as a little trickle from the glacier, and in its swift descent down the mountain slopes it did not give the sun a chance to penetrate its waters. But we were determined to bathe, to wash away the dust and sweat of our two days' trudging, and we leapt about in the shallows like startled porpoises, slapping water on each other, and gasping with the shock of each immersion. Bisnu, more accustomed to mountain streams than ourselves, ventured across in ail attempt to catch an otter, but wasn't fast enough. Then we were on the springy grass, wrestling each other in order to get warm.

The bungalow stood on a ledge just above the river, and the sound of the water rushing down the mountain defile could be heard at all times. The sound of the birds, which we had grown used to, was drowned by the sound of the water; but the birds themselves could be seen, many coloured, standing out splendidly against the dark green forest foliage: the red-crowned jay, the paradise flycatcher, the purple whistling-thrush, others we could not recognize.

Higher up the mountain, above some terraced land where oats and barley were grown, stood a small cluster of huts. This, we were told by the watchman, was the last village on the way to the glacier. It was, in fact, one of the last villages in India, because if we crossed the difficult passes beyond the glacier; we would find ourselves in Tibet. We told the watchman we would be quite satisfied if we reached the glacier.

Then Anil made the mistake of mentioning the Abominable Snowman, of whom we had been reading in the papers. The people of Nepal believe in the existence of the Snowman, and our watchman was a Nepali.

'Yes, I have seen the Yeti,' he told us. 'A great shaggy flat-footed creature. In the winter, when it snows heavily, he passes by the bungalow at night. I have seen his tracks the next morning.'

'Does he come this way in the summer?' I asked anxiously. We were sitting before another of Bisnu's fires, drinking tea with condensed milk, and trying to get through a black, sticky sweet which the watchman had produced from his tin trunk.

'The yeti doesn't come here in the summer,' said the old man. 'But I have seen the Lidini sometimes. You have to be careful of her.'

'What is a Lidini?' asked Kamal.

'Ah!' said the watchman mysteriously. 'You have heard of the Abominable Snowman, no doubt, but there are few who have heard of the Abominable Snowwoman! And yet she is far the more dangerous of the two!'

'What is she like?' asked Anil, and we all craned forward.

'She is of the same height as the Yeti—about seven feet when her back is straight—and her hair is much longer. She has very long teeth and nails. Her feet face inwards, but she can run very fast, especially downhill. If you see a Lidini, and she chases you, always run away in an uphill direction. She tires quickly because of her feet. But when running downhill she has no trouble at all, and you have to be very fast to escape her!'

'Well, we're all good runners,' said Anil with a nervous laugh, 'but it's just a fairy story, I don't believe a word of it.'

'But you *must* believe fairy stories,' I said, remembering a performance of Peter Pan in London, when those in the audience who believed in fairies were asked to clap their hands in order to save Tinker Bell's life. 'Even if they aren't true,' I added, deciding there was a world of difference between Tinker Bell and the Abominable Snowwoman.

'Well, I don't believe there's a Snowman or a Snowwoman!' declared Anil.

The watchman was most offended and refused to tell us anything about the Sagpa and Sagpani; but Bisnu knew, about them, and later, when we were in bed, he told us that they were similar to Snowmen but much smaller. Their favourite pastime was sleeping, and they became very annoyed if anyone woke them, and became ferocious, and did not give one much time to start running uphill. The Sagpa and Sagpani sometimes kidnapped small children, and taking them to their cave, would look after the children very carefully, feeding them on fruits, honey, rice and earthworms.

'When the Sagpa isn't looking,' he said, 'you can throw the earthworms over your shoulder.'

5
The Glacier

It was a fine sunny morning when we set out to cover the last seven miles to the glacier. We had expected this to be a stiff climb, but the last dak bungalow was situated at well over 10,000 feet above sea level, and the ascent was to be fairly gradual.

And suddenly, abruptly, there were no more trees. As the bungalow dropped out of sight, the trees and bushes gave way to short grass and little blue and pink alpine flowers. The snow peaks were close now, ringing us in on every side. We passed waterfalls, cascading hundreds of feet down precipitous rock faces, thundering into the little river.

A great golden eagle hovered over us for some time.

'I feel different again,' said Kamal.

'We're very high now,' I said. 'I hope we won't get headaches.'

'I've got one already,' complained Anil. 'Let's have some tea.'

We had left our cooking utensils at the bungalow, expecting to return there for the night, and had brought with us only a few biscuits, chocolate, and a thermos of tea. We finished the tea, and Bisnu scrambled about on the grassy slopes, collecting wild strawberries. They were tiny strawberries, very sweet, and they did nothing to satisfy our appetites. There was no sign of habitation or human life. The only creatures to be found at that height were the gurals—sure-footed mountain goats—and an occasional snow-leopard, or a bear.

We found and explored a small cave, and then, turning a bend, came unexpectedly upon the glacier.

The hill fell away, and there, confronting us, was a great white field of snow and ice, cradled between two peaks that could only have been the abode of the gods. We were speechless for several minutes. Kamal took my hand and held on to it for reassurance; perhaps he was not sure that what he saw was real. Anil's mouth hung open. Bisnu's eyes glittered with excitement.

We proceeded cautiously on the snow, supporting each other on the slippery surface; but we could not go far, because we were quite unequipped for any high-altitude climbing. It was pleasant to feel that we were the only boys in our town who had climbed so high. A few black rocks jutted out from the snow, and we sat down on them, to feast our eyes on the view. The sun reflected sharply from the snow, and we felt surprisingly warm.

'Let's sunbathe!' said Anil, on a sudden impulse.

'Yes, let's do that!' I said.

In a few minutes we had taken off our clothes and, sitting on the rocks, were exposing ourselves to the elements, It was delicious to feel the sun crawling over my skin. Within half an hour I was postbox red, and so was Bisnu, and the two of us decided to get into our clothes before the sun scorched the skin off our backs. Kamal and Anil appeared to be more resilient to sunlight, and laughed at our discomfiture. Bisnu and I avenged ourselves by gathering up handfuls of snow and rubbing it on their backs. We dressed quickly enough after that, Anil leaping about like a performing monkey.

Meanwhile, almost imperceptibly, clouds had covered some of the peaks, and white mist drifted clown the mountain-slopes. It was time to get back to the bungalow; we would barely make it before dark.

We had not gone far when lightning began to sizzle about the mountain-tops followed by waves of thunder.

'Let's run!' shouted Anil. 'We can shelter in the cave!'

The clouds could hold themselves in no longer, and the rain came down suddenly, stinging our faces as it was whipped up by all icy wind. Half-blinded, we ran as fast as we could along the slippery path, and stumbled, drenched and exhausted, into the little cave.

The cave was mercifully dry, and not very dark. We remained at the entrance, watching the rain sweep past us, listening to the wind whistling down the long gorge.

'It will take some time to stop,' said Kamal.

'No, it will pass soon,' said Bisnu. 'These storms are short and fierce.'

Anil produced his pocket knife, and to pass the time we carved our names in the smooth rock of the cave.

'We will come here again, when we are older,' said Kamal, 'and perhaps our names will still be here.'

It had grown dark by the time the rain stopped. A full moon helped us find our way, we went slowly and carefully. The rain had loosened the earth, and stones kept rolling down the hillside. I was afraid of starting a landslide.

'I hope we don't meet the Lidini now,' said Anil fervently.

'I thought you didn't believe in her,' I said.

'I don't,' replied Anil. 'But what if I'm wrong?'

We saw only a mountain-goat, the gural, poised on the brow of a precipice, silhouetted against the sky. And then the path vanished.

Had it not been for the bright moonlight, we might have walked straight into an empty void. The rain had caused a landslide, and where there had been a narrow path there was now only a precipice of loose, slippery shale.

'We'll have to go back,' said Bisnu. 'It will be too dangerous to try and cross in the dark.'

'We'll sleep in the cave,' I suggested.

'We've nothing to sleep in ,' said Anil. 'Not a single blanket between us and nothing to eat!'

'We'll just have to rough it till morning,' said Kamal.

'It will be better than breaking our necks here.'

We returned to the cave, which did at least have the virtue of being dry. Bisnu had matches, and he made a fire with sonic dry sticks which had been left in the cave by a previous party. We ate what was left of a loaf of bread.

There was no sleep for any of us that night. We lay close to each other for comfort, but the ground was hard and uneven. And every noise we heard outside the cave made us think of leopards and bears and even the Abominable Snowman.

We got up as soon as there was a faint glow in the sky. The snow-peaks were bright pink, but we were too tired and hungry and worried to care for the beauty of the sunrise. We took the path to the landslide, and once again looked for a way across. Kamal ventured to take a few steps on the loose pebbles, but the ground gave way immediately, and we had to grab him by the arms and shoulders to prevent him from sliding a hundred feet clown the gorge.

'Now what are we going to do?' I asked.

'Look for another way,' said Bisnu.

'But do you know of any?'

And we all turned to look at Bisnu, expecting him to provide the solution to our problem.

'I have heard of a way,' said Bisnu, 'but I have never used it. It will be a little dangerous, I think. The path has not been used for several years—not since the traders stopped coming in from Tibet.'

'Never mind, we'll try it,' said Anil.

'We will have to cross the glacier first,' said Bisnu. 'That's the main problem.'

We looked at each other in silence. The glacier didn't look difficult to cross, but we know that it would not be easy for novices. For almost two furlongs it consisted of hard, slippery ice.

Anil was the first to arrive at a decision.

'Come on,' he said. 'There's no time to waste.'

We were soon on the glacier. And we remained on it for a long time. For every two steps forward, we slid one step backward. Our progress was slow and awkward. Sometimes, after advancing several yards across the ice at a steep incline, one of us would slip back and the others would have to slither down to help him up. At one particularly difficult spot, I dropped our water bottle and, grabbing at it, lost my footing, fell full-length and went sliding some twenty feet down the ice-slope.

I had sprained my wrist and hurt my knee, and was to prove a liability for the rest of the trek.

Kamal tied his handkerchief round my hand, and Anil took charge of the water-bottle, which we had filled with ice. Using my good hand to grab Bisnu's legs whenever I slipped, I struggled on behind the others.

It was almost noon, and we were quite famished, when we put our feet on grass again. And then we had another steep climb, clutching at roots and grasses, before we reached the path that Bisnu had spoken about. It was little more than a goat-track, but it took us round the mountain and brought us within sight of the dak bungalow.

'I could eat a whole chicken,' said Kamal.

'I could eat two,' I said.

'I could eat a snowman,' said Bisnu.

'And I could eat the chowkidar,' said Anil.

Fortunately for the chowkidar, he had anticipated our hunger; and when we staggered into the bungalow late in the afternoon, we found a meal waiting for us. True, there was no chicken—but, so ravenous did we feel, that even the lowly onion tasted delicious!

We had Bisnu to thank for getting us back successfully. He had brought us over mountain and glacier with all the skill and confidence of a boy who had the Himalayas in his blood.

We took our time getting back to Kapkote; fished in the Sarayu river; bathed with the village boys we had seen on our way up; collected strawberries and ferns and wild flowers; and finally said goodbye to Bisnu.

Anil wanted to take Bisnu along with us, but the boy's parents refused to let him go, saying that he was too young for the life of a city; but we were of the opinion that Bisnu could have taught the city boys a few things.

'Never mind,' said Kamal. 'We'll go on another trip next year, and we'll take you with us, Bisnu. We'll write and let you know our plans.'

This promise made Bisnu happy, and he saw us off at the bus stop, shouldering our bedding to the end. There he skimmed up the trunk of a fir tree to have a better view of us leaving, and we saw him waving to us from the tree as our bus went round the bend from Kapkote, and the hills were left behind and the plains stretched out below.

Tremors in the Night

Not to be discouraged, we left the ghost town and continued our journey upriver, as far as the bus would take us. The road ended at Uttarkashi, for the simple reason that the bridge over the Bhagirathi had been washed away in a flash flood. The glaciers had been melting, and that, combined with torrential rain in the upper reaches, had brought torrents of muddy water rushing down the swollen river. Anything that came in its way vanished downstream.

We spent the night in a pilgrim shelter, built on a rocky ledge overlooking the river. All night we could hear the water roaring past below us. After a while, we became used to the unchanging sound; it became like a deep silence, and made our sleep deeper. Sometime before dawn, however, a sudden tremor had us trembling out of our cots.

'Earthquake!' shouted Sunil, making for the doorway and banging into the wall instead.

'Don't panic,' I said, feeling panicky.

'It will pass,' said Buddhoo.

The tremor did pass, but not before everyone in the shelter had rushed outside. There was the sound of rocks falling, and everyone rushed back again. 'Landslide!' someone shouted. Was it safer outside or inside? No one could be sure.

'It will pass,' said Buddhoo again, and went to sleep.

Sunil began singing at the top of his voice: '*Pyar kiya to darna kya*—Why be afraid when we have loved'. I doubt Sunil had ever been in love, but it was a rousing song with which to meet death.

'*Chup, beta!*' admonished an old lady on her last pilgrimage to the abode of the gods. 'Say your prayers instead.'

The room fell silent. Outside, a dog started howling. Other dogs followed his example. Not to serenade us, but a mournful anticipation of things to come; for birds and beasts are more sensitive to the earth's tremors and inner convulsions than humans, who are no longer sensitive to nature's warnings.

A couple of jackals joined the chorus. Then a bird, probably a nightjar, set up a monotonous croak. I looked at my watch. It was 4 a.m, a little too early for birds to be greeting the break of day. But suddenly there was a twittering and cawing and chattering as all the birds in the vicinity passed on the message that something was amiss.

There was a rush of air and a window banged open.

The mountain shuddered. The building shook, rocked to and fro.

People began screaming and making for the door.

The door was flung open, but only a few escaped into the darkness.

Across the length of the room a chasm opened up. The lady saying her prayers fell into it. So did one or two others. Then the room and the people in it—those who were on the other side of the chasm—suddenly vanished.

There was the roar of falling masonry as half the building slid down the side of the mountain.

We were left dangling in space.

'Let's get out of here quickly!' shouted Sunil.

We scrambled out of the door. In front of us, an empty void. I couldn't see a thing. Then Buddhoo took me by the hand and led me away from the crumbling building and on to the rocky ledge above the river.

The earth had stopped quaking, but the mountain had been shaken to its foundations, and rocks and trees were tumbling into the swollen river. The town was in darkness, the power station having shut down after the first tremor. Here and there a torch or lantern shone out of the darkness, and people could be heard wailing and shouting to each other as they roamed the streets in the rain. Somewhere a siren went off. It only seemed to add to the panic.

At 5 a.m, the rain stopped and the sky lightened. At six it was daybreak. A little later the sun came up. A beautiful morning, except for the devastation.

Ganga Takes All

'*G*anga-mai ki jai!'

The boat carrying pilgrims across the sacred river was ready to leave. Sunil and I scrambled down the river bank and tumbled into it. It was already overloaded, but we squeezed in amongst the pilgrims, mostly rural folk who had come to Haridwar to visit the temples and take home bottles of Ganga water—in much the same way that the faithful come to Lourdes, in France, and carry away the healing waters of a sacred stream. People are the same everywhere.

In those days there was no road bridge across the Ganga, and the train took one to Bijnor by a long and circuitous route. Sunil's village was off the beaten track, some thirty miles from the nearest station. The easiest way to get there was to cross the river by boat and then take an ekka, or pony-cart, to get to the village.

The boat was meant to take about a dozen people, but for a few rupees more the boatmen would usually take in more than the permitted number. When we set off, there must have been at least twenty in the boat—men, women and children.

'*Ganga-mai ki jai!*' they chanted, as the two oarsmen swung into the current.

For a time, all went well. In spite of its load, the boat made headway, being carried a little downstream but in the general direction of its landing place. Then halfway across the river, where the water was deep and strong, the boat began to wobble about and water slopped in over the sides.

The singing stopped, and a few called out in dismay.

There was little one could do, except urge the oarsmen on.

They did their best, straining at the oars, the sweat pouring down their bare bodies. We made some progress, although we were now drifting with the current.

'It doesn't matter where we land,' I said, 'as long as we don't take in water.'

I had always been nervous in small boats. The fear of drowning had been with me since childhood: I'd seen a dhow go down off the Kathiawar coast, and bodies washed ashore the next day.

'*Ganga-mai ki jai!*' called one or two hardy souls, and we were about two-thirds across the river when water began to fill the boat. The women screamed, the children cried out.

'Don't panic!' I yelled, though filled with panic. 'It's not so deep here, we can get ashore.'

The boat struck a sandbank, tipped over. We were in the water.

I was waist-deep in water, but the current was strong, taking me along. The menfolk picked up the smaller children and struggled to reach the shore. The women struggled to follow them.

Two of the older women were carried downstream; I have no idea what happened to them.

Sunil was splashing about near the capsized boat. 'Where's my suitcase?' he yelled.

I saw it bobbing about on the water, just out of his reach. He made a grab for it, but it was swept away. I saw it disappearing downstream. It might float for a while, then sink to the bottom of the river. No one would find it there. Or some day the suitcase would burst open, its contents carried further downstream, and the emerald bracelet be washed up among the pebbles of the riverbed. A fisherman might find it. In older times he would have taken it to his king. In present times he would keep it.

We struggled ashore with the others and sank down on the sand, exhausted but happy to be alive.

Those who still had some strength left sang out: '*Ganga-mai ki jai!*' And so did I.

Sunil still had the sapphire ring on his hand, but it hadn't done him much good.

How Far Is the River?

Between the boy and the river was a mountain. I was a small boy, and it was a small river, but the mountain was big.

The thickly forested mountain hid the river, but I knew it was there and what it looked like; I had never seen the river with my own eyes, but from the villagers I had heard of it, of the fish in its waters, of its rocks and currents and waterfalls, and it only remained for me to touch the water and know it personally.

I stood in front of our house on the hill opposite the mountain, and gazed across the valley, dreaming of the river. I was barefooted; not because I couldn't afford shoes, but because I felt free with my feet bare, because I liked the feel of warm stones and cool grass, because not wearing shoes saved me the trouble of taking them off.

It was eleven o'clock and I knew my parents wouldn't be home till evening. There was a loaf of bread I could take with me, and on the way I might find some fruit. Here was the chance I had been waiting for; it would not come again for a long time, because it was seldom that my father and mother visited friends for the entire day. If I came back before dark, they wouldn't know where I had been.

I went into the house and wrapped the loaf of bread in a newspaper. Then I closed all the doors and windows.

The path to the river dropped steeply into the valley, then rose and went round the big mountain. It was frequently used by the villagers, woodcutters, milkmen, shepherds, mule drivers—but there were no villages beyond the mountain or near the river.

I passed a woodcutter and asked him how far it was to the river. He was a short, powerful man, with a creased and weathered face, and muscles that stood out in hard lumps.

'Seven miles,' he said. 'Why do you want to know?'

'I am going there,' I said.

'Alone?'

'Of course.'

'It will take you three hours to reach it, and then you have to come back. It will be getting dark, and it is not an easy road.'

'But I'm a good walker,' I said, though I had never walked further than the two miles between our house and my school. I left the woodcutter on the path, and continued down the hill.

It was a dizzy, winding path, and I slipped once or twice and slid into a bush or down a slope of slippery pine needles. The hill was covered with lush green ferns, the trees were entangled in creepers, and a great wild dahlia would suddenly rear its golden head from the leaves and ferns.

Soon I was in the valley, and the path straightened out and then began to rise. I met a girl who was coming from the opposite direction. She held a long curved knife with which she had been cutting grass, and there were rings in her nose and ears and her arms were covered with heavy bangles. The bangles made music when she moved her wrists. It was as though her hands spoke a language of their own.

'How far is it to the river?' I asked.

The girl had probably never been to the river, or she may have been thinking of another one, because she said, 'Twenty miles,' without any hesitation.

I laughed and ran down the path. A parrot screeched suddenly, flew low over my head, a flash of blue and green. It took the course of the path, and I followed its dipping flight, running until the path rose and the bird disappeared amongst the trees.

A trickle of water came down the hillside, and I stopped to drink. The water was cold and sharp but very refreshing. But I was soon thirsty again. The sun was striking the side of the hill, and the dusty path became hotter, the stones scorching my feet. I was sure I had covered half the distance: I had been walking for over an hour.

Presently, I saw another boy ahead of me driving a few goat's down the path.

'How far is the river?' I asked.

The village boy smiled and said, 'Oh, not far, just round the next hill and straight down.

Feeling hungry, I unwrapped my loaf of bread and broke it in two, offering one half to the boy. We sat on the hillside and ate in silence.

When we had finished, we walked on together and began talking; and talking I did not notice the smarting of my feet and the heat of the sun, the distance I had covered and the distance I had yet to cover. But after some time my companion had to take another path, and once more I was on my own.

I missed the village boy; I looked up and down the mountain path but no one else was in sight. My own home was hidden from view by the side of the mountain, and there was no sign of the river. I began to feel discouraged. If someone had been with me, I would not have faltered; but alone, I was conscious of my fatigue and isolation.

But I had come more than half way, and I couldn't turn back; I had to see the river. If I failed, I would always be a little ashamed of the experience. So I walked on, along the hot, dusty, stony path, past stone huts and terraced fields, until there were no more fields or huts, only forest and sun and loneliness. There were no men, and no sign of man's influence-only trees and rocks and grass and small flowers-and silence...

The silence was impressive and a little frightening. There was no movement, except for the bending of grass beneath my feet, and the circling of a hawk against the blind blue of the sky.

Then, as I rounded a sharp bend, I heard the sound of water. I gasped with surprise and happiness, and began to run. I slipped and stumbled, but I kept on running, until I was able to plunge into the snow-cold mountain water.

And the water was blue and white and wonderful.

Angry River

In the middle of the big river, the river that began in the mountains and ended in the sea, was a small island. The river swept round the island, sometimes clawing at its banks, but never going right over it. It was over twenty years since the river had flooded the island, and at that time no one had lived there. But for the last ten years a small hut had stood there, a mud-walled hut with a sloping thatched roof. The hut had been built into a huge rock, so only three of the walls were mud, and the fourth was rock.

Goats grazed on the short grass which grew on the island, and on the prickly leaves of thorn bushes. A few hens followed them about. There was a melon patch and a vegetable patch.

In the middle of the island stood a peepul tree. It was the only tree there.

Even during the Great Flood, when the island had been under water, the tree had stood firm.

It was an old tree. A seed had been carried to the island by a strong wind some fifty years back, had found shelter between two rocks, had taken root there, and had sprung up to give shade and shelter to a small family; and Indians love peepul trees, especially during the hot summer months when the heart-shaped leaves catch the least breath of air and flutter eagerly, fanning those who sit beneath.

A sacred tree, the peepul: the abode of spirits, good and bad. 'Don't yawn when you are sitting beneath the tree,' Grandmother used to warn Sita. 'And if you must yawn, always snap your fingers in front of your mouth. If you forget to do that, a spirit might jump down your throat!'

'And then what will happen?' asked Sita.

'It will probably ruin your digestion,' said Grandfather, who wasn't much of a believer in spirits.

The peepul had a beautiful leaf, and Grandmother likened it to the body of the mighty god Krishna—broad at the shoulders, then tapering down to a very slim waist.

It was an old tree, and an old man sat beneath it.

He was mending a fishing net. He had fished in the river for ten years, and he was a good fisherman. He knew where to find the slim silver Chilwa fish and the big beautiful Mahseer and the long-moustached Singhara; he knew where the river was deep and where it was shallow; he knew which baits to use—which fish liked worms and which liked gram. He had taught his son to fish, but his son had gone to work in a factory in a city, nearly a hundred miles away. He had no grandson; but he had a granddaughter, Sita, and she could do all the things a boy could do, and sometimes she could do them better. She had lost her mother when she was very small. Grandmother had taught her all the things a girl should know, and she could do these as well as most girls. But neither of her grandparents could read or write, and as a result Sita couldn't read or write either.

There was a school in one of the villages across the river, but Sita had never seen it. There was too much to do on the island.

While Grandfather mended his net, Sita was inside the hut, pressing her Grandmother's forehead, which was hot with fever. Grandmother had been ill for three days and could not eat. She had been ill before, but she had never been so bad. Grandfather had brought her some sweet oranges from the market in the nearest town, and she could suck the juice from the oranges, but she couldn't eat anything else.

She was younger than Grandfather, but because she was sick, she looked much older. She had never been very strong.

When Sita noticed that Grandmother had fallen asleep, she tiptoed out of the room on her bare feet and stood outside.

The sky was dark with monsoon clouds. It had rained all night, and in a few hours it would rain again. The monsoon rains had come early, at the end of June. Now it was the middle of July, and already the river was swollen. Its rushing sound seemed nearer and more menacing than usual.

Sita went to her grandfather and sat down beside him beneath the peepul tree.

'When you are hungry, tell me,' she said, 'and I will make the bread.'

'Is your grandmother asleep?'

'She sleeps. But she will wake soon, for she has a deep pain.'

The old man stared out across the river, at the dark green of the forest, at the grey sky, and said, 'Tomorrow, if she is not better, I will take her to the hospital at Shahganj. There they will know how to make her well. You may be on your own for a few days—but you have been on your own before…'

Sita nodded gravely; she had been alone before, even during the rainy season. Now she wanted Grandmother to get well, and she knew that only Grandfather had the skill to take the small dugout boat across the river when the current was so strong. Someone would have to stay behind to look after their few possessions.

Sita was not afraid of being alone, but she did not like the look of the river. That morning, when she had gone down to fetch water, she had noticed that the level had risen. Those rocks which were normally spattered with the droppings of snipe and curlew and other waterbirds had suddenly disappeared.

They disappeared every year—but not so soon, surely?

'Grandfather, if the river rises, what will I do?'

'You will keep to the high ground.'

'And if the water reaches the high ground?'

'Then take the hens into the hut, and stay there.'

'And if the water comes into the hut?'

'Then climb into the peepul tree. It is a strong tree. It will not fall. And the water cannot rise higher than the tree!'

'And the goats, Grandfather?'

'I will be taking them with me, Sita. I may have to sell them to pay for good food and medicines for your grandmother. As for the hens, if it becomes necessary, put them on the roof. But do not worry too much'—and he patted Sita's head—'the water will not rise as high. I will be back soon, remember that.'

'And won't Grandmother come back?'

'Yes, of course, but they may keep her in the hospital for some time.'

~

Towards evening, it began to rain again—big pellets of rain, scarring the surface of the river. But it was warm rain, and Sita could move about in it. She was not afraid of getting wet, she rather liked it. In the previous month, when the first monsoon shower had arrived, washing the dusty leaves of the tree and bringing up the good smell of the earth, she had exulted in it, had run about shouting for joy. She was used to it now, and indeed a little tired of the rain, but she did not mind getting wet. It was steamy indoors, and her thin dress would soon dry in the heat from the kitchen fire.

She walked about barefooted, barelegged. She was very sure on her feet; her toes had grown accustomed to gripping all kinds of rocks, slippery or sharp. And though thin, she was surprisingly strong.

Black hair, streaming across her face. Black eyes. Slim brown arms. A scar on her thigh—when she was small, visiting her mother's village, a hyaena had entered the house where she was sleeping, fastened on to her leg and tried to drag her away, but her screams had roused the villagers and the hyaena had run off.

She moved about in the pouring rain, chasing the hens into a shelter behind the hut. A harmless brown snake, flooded out of its hole, was moving across the open ground. Sita picked up a stick, scooped the snake up, and dropped it between a cluster of rocks. She had no quarrel with snakes. They kept down the rats and the frogs. She wondered how the rats had first come to the island—probably in someone's boat, or in a sack of grain. Now it was a job to keep their numbers down.

When Sita finally went indoors, she was hungry. She ate some dried peas and warmed up some goat's milk.

Grandmother woke once and asked for water, and Grandfather held the brass tumbler to her lips.

~

It rained all night.

The roof was leaking, and a small puddle formed on the floor. They kept the kerosene lamp alight. They did not need the light, but somehow it made them feel safer.

The sound of the river had always been with them, although they were seldom aware of it; but that night they noticed a change in its sound. There was something like a moan, like a wind in the tops of tall trees and a swift hiss as the water swept round the rocks and carried away pebbles. And sometimes there was a rumble, as loose earth fell into the water.

Sita could not sleep.

She had a rag doll, made with Grandmother's help out of bits of old clothing. She kept it by her side every night. The doll was someone to talk to, when the nights were long and sleep elusive. Her grandparents were often ready to talk—and Grandmother, when she was well, was a good storyteller—but sometimes Sita wanted to have secrets, and though there were no special secrets in her life, she made up a few, because it was fun to have them. And if you have secrets, you must have a friend to share them with, a companion of one's own age. Since there were no other children on the island, Sita shared her secrets with the rag doll whose name was Mumta.

Grandfather and Grandmother were asleep, though the

sound of Grandmother's laboured breathing was almost as persistent as the sound of the river.

'Mumta,' whispered Sita in the dark, starting one of her private conversations. 'Do you think Grandmother will get well again?'

Mumta always answered Sita's questions, even though the answers could only be heard by Sita.

'She is very old,' said Mumta.

'Do you think the river will reach the hut?' asked Sita.

'If it keeps raining like this, and the river keeps rising, it will reach the hut.'

'I am a little afraid of the river, Mumta. Aren't you afraid?'

'Don't be afraid. The river has always been good to us.'

'What will we do if it comes into the hut?'

'We will climb onto the roof.'

'And if it reaches the roof?'

'We will climb the peepul tree. The river has never gone higher than the peepul tree.'

As soon as the first light showed through the little skylight, Sita got up and went outside. It wasn't raining hard, it was drizzling, but it was the sort of drizzle that could continue for days, and it probably meant that heavy rain was falling in the hills where the river originated.

Sita went down to the water's edge. She couldn't find her favourite rock, the one on which she often sat dangling her feet in the water, watching the little Chilwa fish swim by. It was still there, no doubt, but the river had gone over it.

She stood on the sand, and she could feel the water oozing and bubbling beneath her feet.

The river was no longer green and blue and flecked with white, but a muddy colour.

She went back to the hut. Grandfather was up now. He was getting his boat ready.

Sita milked the goat. Perhaps it was the last time she would milk it.

~

The sun was just coming up when Grandfather pushed off in the boat. Grandmother lay in the prow. She was staring hard at Sita, trying to speak, but the words would not come. She raised her hand in a blessing.

Sita bent and touched her grandmother's feet, and then Grandfather pushed off. The little boat—with its two old people and three goats—riding swiftly on the river, moved slowly, very slowly, towards the opposite bank. The current was so swift now that Sita realized the boat would be carried about half a mile downstream before Grandfather could get it to dry land.

It bobbed about on the water, getting smaller and smaller, until it was just a speck on the broad river.

And suddenly Sita was alone.

There was a wind, whipping the raindrops against her face; and there was the water, rushing past the island; and there was the distant shore, blurred by rain; and there was the small hut; and there was the tree.

Sita got busy. The hens had to be fed. They weren't bothered about anything except food. Sita threw them handfuls of coarse grain and potato peelings and peanut shells.

Then she took the broom and swept out the hut, lit the

charcoals burner, warmed some milk and thought, 'Tomorrow there will be no milk...' She began peeling onions. Soon her eyes started smarting and, pausing for a few moments and glancing round the quiet room, she became aware again that she was alone. Grandfather's hookah pipe stood by itself in one corner. It was a beautiful old hookah, which had belonged to Sita's great-grandfather. The bowl was made out of a coconut encased in silver. The long winding stem was at least four feet in length. It was their most valuable possession. Grandmother's sturdy Shisham-wood walking stick stood in another corner.

Sita looked around for Mumta, found the doll beneath the cot, and placed her within sight and hearing.

Thunder rolled down from the hills. BOOM—BOOM—BOOM...

'The gods of the mountains are angry,' said Sita. 'Do you think they are angry with me?'

'Why should they be angry with you?' asked Mumta.

'They don't have to have a reason for being angry. They are angry with everything, and we are in the middle of everything. We are so small—do you think they know we are here?'

'Who knows what the gods think?'

'But I made you,' said Sita, 'and I know you are here.'

'And will you save me if the river rises?'

'Yes, of course. I won't go anywhere without you, Mumta.'

Sita couldn't stay indoors for long. She went out, taking Mumta with her, and stared out across the river, to the safe land on the other side. But was it safe there? The river looked much wider now. Yes, it had crept over its banks and spread far across the flat plain. Far away, people were driving their cattle through waterlogged, flooded fields, carrying their belongings in bundles on their heads or shoulders, leaving their homes, making for the high land. It wasn't safe anywhere.

She wondered what had happened to Grandfather and Grandmother. If they had reached the shore safely, Grandfather would have to engage a bullock cart, or a pony-drawn carriage, to get Grandmother to the district town, five or six miles away, where there was a market, a court, a jail, a cinema and a hospital.

She wondered if she would ever see Grandmother again. She had done her best to look after the old lady, remembering the times when Grandmother had looked after her, had gently touched her fevered brow and had told her stories—stories about the gods: about the young Krishna, friend of birds and animals, so full of mischief, always causing confusion among the other gods; and Indra, who made the thunder and lightning; and Vishnu, the preserver of all good things, whose steed was a great white bird; and Ganesh, with the elephant's head; and Hanuman, the monkey-god, who helped the young Prince Rama in his war with the King of Ceylon. Would Grandmother return to tell her more about them, or would she have to find out for herself?

The island looked much smaller now. In parts, the mud banks had dissolved quickly, sinking into the river. But in the middle of the island there was rocky ground, and the rocks would never crumble, they could only be submerged. In a space in the middle of the rocks grew the tree.

Sita climbed into the tree to get a better view. She had climbed the tree many times and it took her only a few seconds to reach the higher branches. She put her hand to her eyes to shield them from the rain, and gazed upstream.

There was water everywhere. The world had become one vast river. Even the trees on the forested side of the river looked as though they had grown from the water, like mangroves. The sky was banked with massive, moisture-laden clouds. Thunder rolled down from the hills and the river seemed to take it up with a hollow booming sound.

Something was floating down with the current, something big and bloated. It was closer now, and Sita could make out the bulky object—a drowned buffalo, being carried rapidly downstream.

So the water had already inundated the villages further upstream. Or perhaps the buffalo had been grazing too close to the rising river.

Sita's worst fears were confirmed when, a little later, she saw planks of wood, small trees and bushes, and then a wooden bedstead, floating past the island.

How long would it take for the river to reach her own small hut?

As she climbed down from the tree, it began to rain more heavily. She ran indoors, shooing the hens before her. They flew into the hut and huddled under Grandmother's cot. Sita thought it would be best to keep them together now. And having them with her took away some of the loneliness.

There were three hens and a cock bird. The river did not bother them. They were interested only in food, and Sita kept them happy by throwing them a handful of onion skins.

She would have liked to close the door and shut out the swish of the rain and the boom of the river, but then she would have no way of knowing how fast the water rose.

She took Mumta in her arms, and began praying for the rain to stop and the river to fall. She prayed to the god Indra, and, just in case he was busy elsewhere, she prayed to other gods too. She prayed for the safety of her grandparents and for her own safety. She put herself last but only with great difficulty.

She would have to make herself a meal. So she chopped up some onions, fried them, then added turmeric and red chilli powder and stirred until she had everything sizzling; then she added a tumbler of water, some salt, and a cup of one of the cheaper lentils. She covered the pot and allowed the mixture to simmer.

Doing this took Sita about ten minutes. It would take at least half an hour for the dish to be ready.

When she looked outside, she saw pools of water amongst the rocks and near the tree. She couldn't tell if it was rain water or overflow from the river.

She had an idea.

A big tin trunk stood in a corner of the room. It had belonged to Sita's mother. There was nothing in it except a cotton-filled quilt, for use during the cold weather. She would stuff the trunk with everything useful or valuable, and weigh it down so that it wouldn't be carried away, just in case the river came over the island.

Grandfather's hookah went into the trunk. Grandmother's walking stick went in too. So did a number of small tins containing the spices used in cooking—nutmeg, caraway seed, cinnamon, coriander and pepper—a bigger tin of flour and a tin of raw sugar. Even if Sita had to spend several hours in the tree, there would be something to eat when she came down again.

A clean white cotton shirt of Grandfather's, and Grandmother's only spare sari also went into the trunk. Never mind if they got stained with yellow curry powder! Never mind if they got to smell of salted fish, some of that went in too.

Sita was so busy packing the trunk that she paid no attention to the lick of cold water at her heels. She locked the trunk, placed the key high on the rock wall, and turned to give her attention to the lentils. It was only then that she discovered that she was walking about on a watery floor.

She stood still, horrified by what she saw. The water was oozing over the threshold, pushing its way into the room.

Sita was filled with panic. She forgot about her meal and everything else. Darting out of the hut, she ran splashing through ankle-deep water towards the safety of the peepul tree. If the tree hadn't been there, such a well-known landmark, she might have floundered into deep water, into the river.

She climbed swiftly into the strong arms of the tree, made herself secure on a familiar branch, and thrust the wet hair away from her eyes.

~

She was glad she had hurried. The hut was now surrounded by water. Only the higher parts of the island could still be seen—a few rocks, the big rock on which the hut was built, a hillock on which some thorny bilberry bushes grew.

The hens hadn't bothered to leave the hut. They were probably perched on the cot now.

Would the river rise still higher? Sita had never seen it like this before. It swirled around her, stretching in all directions.

More drowned cattle came floating down. The most unusual things went by on the water—an aluminium kettle, a cane chair, a tin of tooth powder, an empty cigarette packet, a wooden slipper, a plastic doll...

A doll!

With a sinking feeling, Sita remembered Mumta.

Poor Mumta! She had been left behind in the hut. Sita, in her hurry, had forgotten her only companion.

Well, thought Sita, if I can be careless with someone I've made, how can I expect the gods to notice me, alone in the middle of the river?

The waters were higher now, the island fast disappearing.

Something came floating out of the hut.

It was an empty kerosene tin, with one of the hens perched on top. The tin came bobbing along on the water, not far from the tree, and was then caught by the current and swept into the river. The hen still managed to keep its perch.

A little later, the water must have reached the cot because the remaining hens flew up to the rock ledge and sat huddled there in the small recess.

The water was rising rapidly now, and all that remained of the island was the big rock that supported the hut, the top of the hut itself and the peepul tree.

It was a tall tree with many branches and it seemed unlikely that the water could ever go right over it. But how long would Sita have to remain there? She climbed a little higher, and as she did so, a jet-black jungle crow settled in the upper branches, and Sita saw that there was a nest in them—a crow's nest, an untidy platform of twigs wedged in the fork of a branch.

In the nest were four blue-green, speckled eggs. The crow sat on them and cawed disconsolately. But though the crow was miserable, its presence brought some cheer to Sita. At least she was not alone. Better to have a crow for company than no one at all.

Other things came floating out of the hut—a large pumpkin; a red turban belonging to Grandfather, unwinding in the water like a long snake; and then—Mumta!

The doll, being filled with straw and wood-shavings, moved quite swiftly on the water and passed close to the peepul tree. Sita saw it and wanted to call out, to urge her friend to make for the tree, but she knew that Mumta could not swim—the doll could only float, travel with the river, and perhaps be washed ashore many miles downstream.

The tree shook in the wind and the rain. The crow cawed and flew up, circled the tree a few times and returned to the nest. Sita clung to her branch.

The tree trembled throughout its tall frame. To Sita it felt like an earthquake tremor; she felt the shudder of the tree in her own bones.

The river swirled all around her now. It was almost up to the roof of the hut. Soon the mud walls would crumble and vanish. Except for the big rock and some trees far, far away, there was only water to be seen.

For a moment or two Sita glimpsed a boat with several people in it moving sluggishly away from the ruins of a flooded village, and she thought she saw someone pointing towards her, but the river swept them on and the boat was lost to view.

The river was very angry; it was like a wild beast, a dragon on the rampage, thundering down from the hills and sweeping across the plain, bringing with it dead animals, uprooted trees, household goods and huge fish choked to death by the swirling mud.

The tall old peepul tree groaned. Its long, winding roots clung tenaciously to the earth from which the tree had sprung many, many years ago. But the earth was softening, the stones were being washed away. The roots of the tree were rapidly losing their hold.

The crow must have known that something was wrong, because it kept flying up and circling the tree, reluctant to settle in it and reluctant to fly away. As long as the nest was there, the crow would remain, flapping about and cawing in alarm.

Sita's wet cotton dress clung to her thin body. The rain ran down from her long black hair. It poured from every leaf of the tree. The crow, too, was drenched and groggy.

The tree groaned and moved again. It had seen many monsoons. Once before, it had stood firm while the river had swirled around its massive trunk. But it had been young then.

Now, old in years and tired of standing still, the tree was ready to join the river.

With a flurry of its beautiful leaves, and a surge of mud from below, the tree left its place in the earth, and, tilting, moved slowly forward, turning a little from side to side, dragging its roots along the ground. To Sita, it seemed as though the river was rising to meet the sky. Then the tree moved into the main current of the river, and went a little faster, swinging Sita from side to side. Her feet were in the water but she clung tenaciously to her branch.

~

The branches swayed, but Sita did not lose her grip. The water was very close now. Sita was frightened. She could not see the extent of the flood or the width of the river. She could only see the immediate danger—the water surrounding the tree.

The crow kept flying around the tree. The bird was in a terrible rage. The nest was still in the branches, but not for long... The tree lurched and twisted slightly to one side, and the nest fell into the water. Sita saw the eggs go one by one.

The crow swooped low over the water, but there was nothing it could do. In a few moments, the nest had disappeared.

The bird followed the tree for about fifty yards, as though hoping that something still remained in the tree. Then, flapping its wings, it rose high into the air and flew across the river until it was out of sight.

Sita was alone once more. But there was no time for feeling lonely. Everything was in motion—up and down and sideways and forwards. 'Any moment,' thought Sita, 'the tree will turn right over and I'll be in the water!'

She saw a turtle swimming past—a great river turtle, the kind that feeds on decaying flesh. Sita turned her face away. In the distance, she saw a flooded village and people in flat-bottomed boats but they were very far away.

Because of its great size, the tree did not move very swiftly on the river. Sometimes, when it passed into shallow water, it stopped, its roots catching in the rocks; but not for long—the river's momentum soon swept it on.

At one place, where there was a bend in the river, the tree struck a sandbank and was still.

Sita felt very tired. Her arms were aching and she was no longer upright. With the tree almost on its side, she had to cling tightly to her branch to avoid falling off. The grey weeping sky was like a great shifting dome.

She knew she could not remain much longer in that position. It might be better to try swimming to some distant rooftop or tree. Then she heard someone calling. Craning her neck to look upriver, she was able to make out a small boat coming directly towards her.

The boat approached the tree. There was a boy in the boat who held on to one of the branches to steady himself, giving his free hand to Sita.

She grasped it, and slipped into the boat beside him.

The boy placed his bare foot against the tree trunk and pushed away.

The little boat moved swiftly down the river. The big tree was left far behind. Sita would never see it again.

~

She lay stretched out in the boat, too frightened to talk. The boy looked at her, but he did not say anything, he did not even smile. He lay on his two small oars, stroking smoothly, rhythmically, trying to keep from going into the middle of the river. He wasn't strong enough to get the boat right out of the swift current, but he kept trying.

A small boat on a big river—a river that had no boundaries but which reached across the plains in all directions. The boat moved swiftly on the wild waters, and Sita's home was left far behind.

The boy wore only a loincloth. A sheathed knife was knotted into his waistband. He was a slim, wiry boy, with a hard flat belly; he had high cheekbones, strong white teeth. He was a little darker than Sita.

'You live on the island,' he said at last, resting on his oars and allowing the boat to drift a little, for he had reached a broader, more placid stretch of the river. 'I have seen you sometimes. But where are the others?'

'My grandmother was sick,' said Sita, 'so Grandfather took her to the hospital in Shahganj.'

'When did they leave?'

'Early this morning.'

Only that morning—and yet it seemed to Sita as though it had been many mornings ago.

'Where have you come from?' she asked. She had never seen the boy before.

'I come from...' he hesitated, '...near the foothills. I was in my boat, trying to get across the river with the news that one of the villages was badly flooded, but the current was too strong. I was swept down past your island. We cannot fight the river, we must go wherever it takes us.'

'You must be tired. Give me the oars.'

'No. There is not much to do now, except keep the boat steady.'

He brought in one oar, and with his free hand he felt under the seat where there was a small basket. He produced two mangoes, and gave one to Sita.

They bit deep into the ripe fleshy mangoes, using their teeth to tear the skin away. The sweet juice trickled down their chins. The flavour of the fruit was heavenly—truly this was the nectar of the gods! Sita hadn't tasted a mango for over a year. For a few moments she forgot about the flood—all that mattered was the mango!

The boat drifted, but not so swiftly now, for as they went further away across the plains, the river lost much of its tremendous force.

'My name is Krishan,' said the boy. 'My father has many cows and buffaloes, but several have been lost in the flood.'

'I suppose you go to school,' said Sita.

'Yes, I am supposed to go to school. There is one not far from our village. Do you have to go to school?'

'No—there is too much work at home.'

It was no use wishing she was at home—home wouldn't be there any more—but she wished, at that moment, that she had another mango.

Towards evening, the river changed colour. The sun, low in the sky, emerged from behind the clouds, and the river changed slowly from grey to gold, from gold to a deep orange, and then, as the sun went down, all these colours were drowned in the river, and the river took on the colour of the night.

The moon was almost at the full and Sita could see across the river, to where the trees grew on its banks.

'I will try to reach the trees,' said the boy, Krishan. 'We do not want to spend the night on the water, do we?'

And so he pulled for the trees. After ten minutes of strenuous rowing, he reached a turn in the river and was able to escape the pull of the main current.

Soon they were in a forest, rowing between tall evergreens.

~

They moved slowly now, paddling between the trees, and the moon lighted their way, making a crooked silver path over the water.

'We will tie the boat to one of these trees,' said Krishan. 'Then we can rest. Tomorrow we will have to find our way out of the forest.'

He produced a length of rope from the bottom of the boat, tied one end to the boat's stern and threw the other end over a stout branch which hung only a few feet above the water. The boat came to rest against the trunk of the tree.

It was a tall, sturdy Toon tree—the Indian mahogany—and it was quite safe, for there was no rush of water here; besides, the trees grew close together, making the earth firm and unyielding.

But the denizens of the forest were on the move. The animals had been flooded out of their holes, caves and lairs, and were looking for shelter and dry ground.

Sita and Krishan had barely finished tying the boat to the tree when they saw a huge python gliding over the water towards them. Sita was afraid that it might try to get into the boat; but it went past them, its head above water, its great awesome length trailing behind, until it was lost in the shadows.

Krishan had more mangoes in the basket, and he and Sita sucked hungrily on them while they sat in the boat.

A big sambur stag came thrashing through the water. He did not have to swim; he was so tall that his head and shoulders remained well above the water. His antlers were big and beautiful.

'There will be other animals,' said Sita. 'Should we climb into the tree?'

'We are quite safe in the boat,' said Krishan. 'The animals are interested only in reaching dry land. They will not even hunt each other. Tonight, the deer are safe from the panther and the tiger. So lie down and sleep, and I will keep watch.'

Sita stretched herself out in the boat and closed her eyes, and the sound of the water lapping against the sides of the boat soon lulled her to sleep. She woke once, when a strange bird called overhead. She raised herself on one elbow, but Krishan was awake, sitting in the prow, and he smiled reassuringly at her. He looked blue in the moonlight, the colour of the young god Krishna, and for a few moments Sita was confused and wondered if the boy was indeed Krishna; but when she thought about it, she decided that it wasn't possible. He was just a village boy and she had seen hundreds like him—well, not exactly like him; he was different, in a way she couldn't explain to herself...

And when she slept again, she dreamt that the boy and Krishna were one, and that she was sitting beside him on a great white bird which flew over mountains, over the snow peaks of the Himalayas, into the cloud-land of the gods. There was a great rumbling sound, as though the gods were angry about the whole thing, and she woke up to this terrible sound and looked about her, and there in the moonlit glade, up to his belly in water, stood a young elephant, his trunk raised as he trumpeted his predicament to the forest—for he was a young elephant, and he was lost, and he was looking for his mother.

He trumpeted again, and then lowered his head and listened. And presently, from far away, came the shrill trumpeting of another elephant. It must have been the young one's mother, because he gave several excited trumpet calls, and then went stamping and churning through the flood water towards a gap in the trees. The boat rocked in the waves made by his passing.

'It's all right now,' said Krishan. 'You can go to sleep again.'

'I don't think I will sleep now,' said Sita.

'Then I will play my flute for you,' said the boy, 'and the time will pass more quickly.'

From the bottom of the boat he took a flute, and putting it to his lips, he began to play. The sweetest music that Sita had ever heard came pouring from the little flute, and it seemed to fill the forest with its beautiful sound. And the music carried her away again, into the land of dreams, and they were riding on the bird once more, Sita and the blue god, and they were passing through clouds and mist, until suddenly the sun shot out through the clouds. And at the same moment, Sita opened her eyes and saw the sun streaming through the branches of the Toon tree, its bright green leaves making a dark pattern against the blinding blue of the sky.

Sita sat up with a start, rocking the boat. There were hardly any clouds left. The trees were drenched with sunshine.

The boy Krishan was fast asleep in the bottom of the boat. His flute lay in the palm of his half-open hand. The sun came slanting across his bare brown legs. A leaf had fallen on his upturned face, but it had not woken him, it lay on his cheek as though it had grown there.

Sita did not move again. She did not want to wake the boy.

It didn't look as though the water had gone down, but it hadn't risen, and that meant the flood had spent itself.

The warmth of the sun, as it crept up Krishan's body, woke him at last. He yawned, stretched his limbs, and sat up beside Sita.

'I'm hungry,' he said with a smile.

'So am I,' said Sita.

'The last mangoes,' he said, and emptied the basket of its last two mangoes.

After they had finished the fruit, they sucked the big seeds until these were quite dry. The discarded seeds floated well on the water. Sita had always preferred them to paper boats.

'We had better move on,' said Krishan.

He rowed the boat through the trees, and then for about an hour they were passing through the flooded forest, under the dripping branches of rain-washed trees. Sometimes they had to use the oars to push away vines and creepers. Sometimes drowned bushes hampered them. But they were out of the forest before noon.

Now the water was not very deep and they were gliding over flooded fields. In the distance, they saw a village. It was on high ground. In the old days, people had built their villages on hilltops, which gave them a better defence against bandits and invading armies. This was an old village, and though its inhabitants had long ago exchanged their swords for pruning forks, the hill on which it stood now protected it from the flood.

The people of the village—long-limbed, sturdy Jats—were generous, and gave the stranded children food and shelter. Sita was anxious to find her grandparents, and an old farmer who had business in Shahganj offered to take her there. She was hoping that Krishan would accompany her, but he said he would wait in the village, where he knew others would soon be arriving, his own people among them.

'You will be all right now,' said Krishan. 'Your grandfather will be anxious for you, so it is best that you go to him as soon as you can. And in two or three days, the water will go down and you will be able to return to the island.'

'Perhaps the island has gone forever,' said Sita.

As she climbed into the farmer's bullock cart, Krishan handed her his flute.

'Please keep it for me,' he said. 'I will come for it one day.' And when he saw her hesitate, he added, his eyes twinkling, 'It is a good flute!'

~

It was slow going in the bullock cart. The road was awash, the wheels got stuck in the mud, and the farmer, his grown son and Sita had to keep getting down to heave and push in order to free the big wooden wheels. They were still in a foot or two of water. The bullocks were bespattered with mud, and Sita's legs were caked with it.

They were a day and a night in the bullock cart before they reached Shahganj; by that time, Sita, walking down the narrow bazaar of the busy market town, was hardly recognizable.

Grandfather did not recognize her. He was walking stiffly down the road, looking straight ahead of him, and would have walked right past the dusty, dishevelled girl if she had not charged straight at his thin, shaky legs and clasped him around the waist.

'Sita!' he cried, when he had recovered his wind and his balance. 'But how are you here? How did you get off the island? I was so worried—it has been very bad these last two days...'

'Is Grandmother all right?' asked Sita.

But even as she spoke, she knew that Grandmother was no longer with them. The dazed look in the old man's eyes told her as much. She wanted to cry, not for Grandmother, who could suffer no more, but for Grandfather, who looked so helpless and bewildered; she did not want him to be unhappy. She forced back her tears, took his gnarled and trembling hand, and led him down the crowded street. And she knew, then, that it would be on her shoulder that Grandfather would have to lean in the years to come.

They returned to the island after a few days, when the river was no longer in spate. There was more rain, but the worst was over. Grandfather still had two of the goats; it had not been necessary to sell more than one.

He could hardly believe his eyes when he saw that the tree had disappeared from the island—the tree that had seemed as permanent as the island, as much a part of his life as the river itself. He marvelled at Sita's escape. 'It was the tree that saved you,' he said.

'And the boy,' said Sita.

Yes, and the boy.

She thought about the boy, and wondered if she would ever see him again. But she did not think too much, because there was so much to do.

For three nights they slept under a crude shelter made out

of jute bags. During the day, she helped Grandfather rebuild the mud hut. Once again, they used the big rock as a support.

The trunk which Sita had packed so carefully had not been swept off the island, but the water had got into it, and the food and clothing had been spoilt. But Grandfather's hookah had been saved, and, in the evenings, after their work was done and they had eaten the light meal which Sita prepared, he would smoke with a little of his old contentment, and tell Sita about other floods and storms which he had experienced as a boy.

Sita planted a mango seed in the same spot where the peepul tree had stood. It would be many years before it grew into a big tree, but Sita liked to imagine sitting in its branches one day, picking the mangoes straight from the tree, and feasting on them all day. Grandfather was more particular about making a vegetable garden and putting down peas, carrots, gram and mustard.

One day, when most of the hard work had been done and the new hut was almost ready, Sita took the flute which had been given to her by the boy, and walked down to the water's edge and tried to play it. But all she could produce were a few broken notes, and even the goats paid no attention to her music.

Sometimes, Sita thought she saw a boat coming down the river and she would run to meet it; but usually there was no boat, or if there was, it belonged to a stranger or to another fisherman. And so she stopped looking out for boats. Sometimes she thought she heard the music of a flute, but it seemed very distant and she could never tell where the music came from.

Slowly, the rains came to an end. The flood waters had receded, and in the villages people were beginning to till the land again and sow crops for the winter months. There were cattle fairs and wrestling matches. The days were warm and sultry. The water in the river was no longer muddy, and one evening Grandfather brought home a huge Mahseer fish and Sita made it into a delicious curry.

~

Grandfather sat outside the hut, smoking his hookah. Sita was at the far end of the island, spreading clothes on the rocks to dry. One of the goats had followed her. It was the friendlier of the two, and often followed Sita about the island. She had made it a necklace of coloured beads.

She sat down on a smooth rock, and, as she did so, she noticed a small bright object in the sand near her feet. She stooped and picked it up. It was a little wooden toy—a coloured peacock—that must have come down on the river and been swept ashore on the island. Some of the paint had rubbed off, but for Sita, who had no toys, it was a great find. Perhaps it would speak to her, as Mumta had spoken to her.

As she held the toy peacock in the palm of her hand, she thought she heard the flute music again, but she did not look up. She had heard it before, and she was sure that it was all in her mind.

But this time the music sounded nearer, much nearer. There was a soft footfall in the sand. And, looking up, she saw the boy, Krishan, standing over her.

'I thought you would never come,' said Sita.

'I had to wait until the rains were over. Now that I am free, I will come more often. Did you keep my flute?'

'Yes, but I cannot play it properly. Sometimes it plays by itself, I think, but it will not play for me!'

'I will teach you to play it,' said Krishan.

He sat down beside her, and they cooled their feet in the water, which was clear now, reflecting the blue of the sky. You could see the sand and the pebbles of the riverbed.

'Sometimes the river is angry, and sometimes it is kind,' said Sita.

'We are part of the river,' said the boy. 'We cannot live without it.'

It was a good river, deep and strong, beginning in the mountains and ending in the sea. Along its banks, for hundreds of miles, lived millions of people, and Sita was only one small girl among them, and no one had ever heard of her, no one knew her—except for the old man, the boy and the river.

Ferns in Foliage

At the bottom of the hill there is a small rippling stream, its water almost hidden by the bright green, tangled growth along its course. It is only by its sound as it batters over the pebbles, that we become aware of it. Here we came across many plants that delight to grow in such places—wild strawberries, wood sorrel, orchids, violets and dandelions, and a nest of ferns.

The first thing one notices is a beautiful group of ferns growing almost to the water. This is the Lady Fern, whose broad fronds must be four to five feet high, a delicate plant, frail and almost transparent in the fineness of its foliage, and looking so tender that you would think the sun and wind would almost scorch or shrivel it up. But the abundant supply of flowing water keeps these ferns cool and fresh.

When the frosts of winter come, the fronds will crumple up into a heap of brown fragments. But their strength has by that time returned into the thick clump of roots to be stored and used for a still finer group of fronds next year.

In the moist parts of any forest there are sure to be several other kinds of ferns such as the Male Fern, with its strong, upright fronds looking like a large green shuttlecock three feet high. One of the commonest of Indian ferns is the Maidenhair which grows along the west coast and in the Himalayan foothills. During the monsoon, it can be found on almost every wall and rock—a delicate, tender fern, easily torn by the wind.

On the stump of a fallen tree grow the Prickly-toothed Buckler fern and the Broad Buckler fern, whose rootlets penetrate the soft, rotting wood to obtain their moisture. They are hardy, often remaining green all through the winter. The handsome Bracken fern often grows to a height of six or seven feet.

Then there is the lovely Hart's tongue fern, great clumps of which grow beside the forest paths. It has broad, green crinkled fronds and is quite unlike other ferns. If you look at the back of the fronds you will see from the little heaps of rust-coloured spore cases, that this is indeed a fern; all ferns grow their seeds in this way.

There are several hundred varieties of ferns. They are easily pressed and preserved. They may also be grown indoors in pots. But they are loveliest in the open, in cool, damp places, in the depths of the forest or by the side of a mountain stream.

The history of ferns goes back to the mists of antiquity. There was a time when ferns and plants like them filled the earth. It was a wet and dripping time. Flowers would have been of no use at all but spores could carry on their lives in the prevailing dampness. Some ferns grew as large as trees. The falling stems of these mighty tree ferns were floated together by mighty streams, carried away to the sea and buried under sand and mud. The remains of these plants being, thus, shut off from the air, could not rot but were slowly changed into coal. The impressions of leaves and stems of these ferns can be distinctively seen on many pieces of coal.

As the earth became drier, ferns retired to the damp, shady spots in which we now find them. They are a declining family but let us hope they will remain with us for some time, for a forest stream without ferns would be like a maiden whose loveliest tresses have been shorn.

A Marriage of the Waters

In summer the grass on the hills is still a pale yellowish green, tinged with brown, and that is how it remains until the monsoon rains bring new life to everything that subsists on the stony Himalayan soil. And then, for four months, the hills are deep, dark, and emerald bright.

But the other day, taking a narrow path that left the dry Mussoorie ridge to link up with Pari Tibba (Fairy Hill), I ran across a path of lush green grass, and I knew there had to be water there.

The grass was soft and springy, spotted with the crimson of small, wild strawberries. Delicate Maidenhair, my favourite fern, grew from a cluster of moist, glistening rocks. Moving the ferns a little, I discovered the spring, a freshet of clear sparkling water.

I never cease to wonder at the tenacity of water—its ability to make its way through various strata of rock, zigzagging, back tracking, finding space; cunningly discovering faults and fissures in the mountain, and sometimes travelling underground for great distance before emerging into the open. Of course, there's no stopping water. For no matter how tiny that little trickle, it has to go somewhere!

Like this little spring. At first I thought it was too small to go anywhere, that it would dry up at the edge of the path. Then I discovered that the grass remained soft and green for some distance along the verge, and that there was moisture beneath the grass. This wet stretch ended abruptly; but, on looking further, I saw it continued on the other side of the path, after briefly going underground again.

I decided to follow its fortunes as it disappeared beneath a tunnel of tall grass and bracken fern. Slithering down a stony slope, I found myself in a small ravine, and there I discovered that my little spring had grown, having been joined by the waters of another spring bubbling up from beneath a path of primroses.

A short distance away, a spotted forktail stood on a rock, surveying this marriage of the waters. His long, forked tail moved slowly up and down. He paid no attention to me, being totally absorbed in the movements of a water spider. A swift peck, and the spider vanished, completing the bird's breakfast. Thirsty, I cupped my hands and drank a little water. So did the forktail. We had a perennial supply of pure water all to ourselves!

There was now a rivulet to follow, and I continued down the ravine until I came to a small pool that was fed not only by my brook (I was already thinking of it as my very own!) but also by a little cascade of water coming down from a rocky ledge. I climbed a little way up the rocks and entered a small cave, in which there was just enough space for crouching down. Water dripped and trickled off its roof and sides. And most wonderful of all, some of these drops created tiny rainbows, for a ray of sunlight had struck through a crevice in the cave roof making the droplets of moisture radiant with all the colours of the spectrum.

When I emerged from the cave, I saw a pair of pine martens drinking at the pool. As soon as they saw me, they were up and away, bounding across the ravine and into the trees.

The brook was now a small stream, but I could not follow it much farther, because the hill went into a steep decline and the water tumbled over large, slippery boulders, becoming a waterfall and then a noisy little torrent as it sped toward the valley.

Climbing up the sides of the ravine to the spur of Pari Tibba, I could see the distant silver of a meandering river and I knew my little stream was destined to become part of it; and that the river would be joined by another that could be seen slipping over the far horizon, and that their combined waters would enter the great Ganga, or Ganges, farther downstream.

This mighty river would, in turn, wander over the rich alluvial plains of northern India, finally flowing into the ocean near the Bay of Bengal.

And the ocean, what was it but another droplet in the universe, in the greater scheme of things? No greater than the glistening drop of water that helped start it all, where the grass grows greener around my little spring on the mountain.